Cal let o
through hi...
out by ...
...**dden**...
...**is litt**... ...**trac**...
tiny child. *My nephew.*

'Is he all right?' Tess's weary voice asked the universal question.

He tried to speak, but the words felt trapped and he coughed to clear his throat. 'We've got a baby boy, here.' He placed the baby into Tess's exhausted arms, so she could snuggle the child against her chest and warm him with her body heat.

Tess glanced up, smiling, and immediately reached out her hand, gripping his forearm. 'Thank you *so* much for being here, for catching Oscar. I couldn't have done it without you.'

The rays of her radiant beam flowed over Cal like spring sunshine, warming him in places he hadn't known had been cold.

'I wouldn't have missed this for anything.' His words came out spontaneously, their truth catching him by surprise. Two days ago he hadn't even met Tess, had had no idea his nephew existed, and now he'd delivered him safely into the world. The feeling was indescribable.

Dear Reader

The definition of family is something that is continually evolving. In some countries, especially in rural communities, a family is multigenerational, living and working together on the land. In Australia in the 1950s 'family' usually referred to the nuclear family—two parents and a couple of kids or more.

Today, the word 'family' is accepted as meaning any combination of related adults and children—sole parent and child, grandparents raising grandchildren, single sex couples raising children, and couples adopting children from overseas. Some couples face more obstacles than others in creating their longed-for family, and that is how the idea for THE SURGEON'S SPECIAL DELIVERY came about.

I hope you enjoy Tess and Callum's story as they deal with a life-altering event that throws them together in ways they could never have imagined. The fall-out is challenging, cataclysmic and life-affirming.

Write and let me know what you think: fiona@fionalowe.com

Happy reading!

Love

Fiona x

THE SURGEON'S SPECIAL DELIVERY

BY
FIONA LOWE

™ MILLS & BOON®
Pure reading pleasure™

First published in Great Britain 2009
Harlequin Mills & Boon Limited,
Eton House, 18-24 Paradise Road, Richmond, Surrey TW9 1SR

© Fiona Lowe 2009

ISBN: 978 0 263 86845 6

Set in Times Roman 10½ on 12¼ pt
03-0509-46268

Printed and bound in Spain
by Litografia Rosés, S.A., Barcelona

Always an avid reader, **Fiona Lowe** decided to combine her love of romance with her interest in all things medical, so writing Medical™ Romance was an obvious choice! She lives in a seaside town in southern Australia, where she juggles writing, reading, working and raising two gorgeous sons, with the support of her own real-life hero! You can visit Fiona's website at www.fionalowe.com

Recent titles by the same author:

THE FRENCH DOCTOR'S MIDWIFE BRIDE
THE SURGEON'S CHOSEN WIFE
HER MIRACLE BABY
THE NURSE'S LONGED-FOR FAMILY
PREGNANT ON ARRIVAL

To Paul for his enthusiastic help, technical details, poetic descriptions and his friendship.

And to Cameron and Andrew for always patiently answering my questions—it's much appreciated!

PROLOGUE

'IT'S a boy.'

The radiographer directed the pointer to the telling piece of anatomy on the ultrasound screen, as the fuzzy grey and white image of a baby floating lazily in its cocoon of fluid came into focus.

A squeal of joy erupted, bouncing off the white hospital walls and embracing every person in the room.

From her prone position on the examination table, Tess Dalton smiled up at the ecstatic couple that squeezed her hands tightly as they kissed each other over her rounded pregnant belly.

Tess's heart threatened to explode from elation. The two people she loved most in the world were finally going to have the child they'd waited so long for, and she was part of this gift of life to them. Part of their family. It was the most fantastic experience of her life.

She grinned. 'So, I'm going to have an honorary nephew. I'll have to learn boy things.'

The couple immediately broke apart and dropped down to her level, simultaneously kissing her on both cheeks, their tears of happiness dampening her skin.

James Halroyd was the first to pull away, clearing his throat gruffly. 'Just as well you're up for the job of honorary auntie, Tess, because his biological uncle isn't exactly the "kick a footy to the kid" type of guy. He's too busy off saving the world.'

Carolyn Halroyd wiped her eyes and patted Tess's swollen belly. 'Oh, Tess, we can't thank you enough for being our surrogate.'

Tess squeezed her best friend's hand. 'I'm honoured to do it. Besides, you're the sister I never had. Without you I wouldn't have even finished high school, let alone qualified as a doctor, so stop thanking me. I should be the one thanking you.'

Carolyn gave a giant sniff and a watery smile. 'You're going to be the best auntie Oscar could ever have.'

'Oscar.' Tess patted her stomach, the newly named foetus immediately morphing into his own personality. 'One thing is for sure, kid, you're going to grow up surrounded by love.'

CHAPTER ONE

'DOCTOR, I have bad news.'

Callum Halroyd's talented hands stilled on the mess that had until an hour ago been a young man's leg, but that had been before a mortar had shattered it into pulp. This was Cal's fifth operation since dawn and the sun had only just hit its highest point. As an experienced surgeon with Frontline Aid, and with the muffled explosions of war sounding in the distance, he was pretty certain he'd still be operating when dusk had disappeared into darkness.

He glanced up over the top of his surgical mask, his mouth twitching into a smile. He always smiled when he saw Jenny Patton. An experienced Frontline nurse, she had the typical dry Australian wit that described every situation in ironic understatement. 'Don't tell me, we've run out of coffee.'

Fully scrubbed, she walked over to him, her usually laughing hazel eyes strangely sombre. 'The coffee supply is safe.'

'That's good to know.' But a streak of cold shot through him quickly, its tendrils remaining, hovering like mist. He shrugged off the feeling and blasted a bleeding capillary with heat from the diathermy.

She stepped in next to him, dextrously applying suction to keep the bloodied area clear. 'Jenson Armand's scrubbing in for you. He's just gloving up now.'

The quipping Jenny had vanished. The cold started to circle his heart. 'What the hell for? I have more vascular experience than he does.' He thrust out his hand. 'More packs.' The words shot from his mouth more like a command than a request as he tried to push his mounting unease aside.

Jenny handed him the gauze, her gaze seeking his. 'I'm really sorry, Cal, there's no easy way to tell you this.' She sighed out a long breath before breathing in deeply. 'We've just heard from Australia. Your brother, James, he was in an accident and he's…'

The circling cold turned into an icy grip, snatching at his heart. 'He's what?'

She blinked rapidly. 'He died yesterday, along with his wife. You need to go home. I've got you on a helicopter out of here to connect with an international flight. You leave in thirty minutes.'

The roar of blood in his head instantly drowned out the sounds of gunfire. His hands shook as he deftly created a stump for a future prosthesis.

James was dead. His brain struggled to come to terms with the fact that his twin brother no longer lived.

'You'll be home in twenty-four hours,' Jenny reassured him. 'Your parents will meet you at Melbourne Airport.'

Home. He shook his head. At some point in the last few years Australia had ceased to be home. Instead, it had become a place to visit on holidays, and now it was calling him back for a funeral. He wasn't sure Australia could ever be home again.

Tess wandered around Carolyn and James's strangely quiet house, desperately missing the aroma of freshly brewed coffee, the hum of Carolyn's sewing machine and the happy off-key whistle that meant James was close at hand. Blinking back tears, she sat down hard on the couch and cradled her very pregnant belly. 'Oh, baby boy, life is so not fair.'

She knew all about 'not fair' but she'd hoped this child wouldn't have to experience it. Leaning back into the soft cushions, she tried to marshal her chaotic thoughts as fatigue broke over her like surf. The outback township of Narranbool had ground to a halt, united in its grief for its beloved GP and his talented wife Carolyn, who had dressed them so stylishly for weddings, debuts, the Narranbool Cup and every other social occasion in between. No matter what their height, weight or proportions, Carolyn's skill had been making everyone look and feel gorgeous.

Tomorrow's funeral had been organised from Melbourne by James's family, but the town had taken control of the wake, needing to show their love and appreciation for two very special people. Tess knew that in true country style grief would be well fed with cream sponges, pavlova, asparagus rolls and tea.

She rubbed her belly as Oscar kicked hard against her hand. Carolyn had no known relatives, but James had parents. Parents who didn't yet know about their unborn grandson.

Tess had to tell them but had balked at doing it over the phone. *Hi, I'm Tess. You don't know me and by the way I'm pregnant with your grandson but I'm not the biological mother.* No, it was something she had to do in person when the Halroyds arrived in town. She'd do it tomorrow, immediately after the funeral.

Organised...by James's family. Being organised by James's family was something she was going to have to deal with. A long sigh shuddered out of her lungs as she tried to give herself a pep talk. Giving up Oscar to his grandparents was no different from giving him up to Carolyn and James.

Yes it is! A traitorous thought that had been gaining volume for two days thundered inside her head.

Pulling herself together, she stared it down hard.

For two days she'd experienced fantasy moments of pretending that Oscar was her own baby. But, of course, he wasn't. He was a Halroyd and she couldn't deny Oscar his birthright. She knew what it was like to grow up without a family. She was intimate with that sense of needing to belong to someone and never having that need filled.

Carolyn and James had been her family for three short years but now they were gone. Their child grew inside her belly, but as a surrogate she had to give him up to his biological family, severing the last connection she had with her dearest friends. Perhaps severing the connection with a child she'd expected to watch grow up and have over for sleepovers. She would fight to stay in touch but what real claim did she have?

Her fragile cocoon of happiness, spun over the last year, had splintered into jagged shards the moment the road train had ploughed headlong into James and Carolyn's car.

Her throat tightened for the hundredth time that day and she blew out a long breath. Thankfully, dealing with the Halroyds was another sixteen hours away. Far enough away to pretend it might not happen, that Oscar could still be hers. 'Tomorrow never comes, right, mate?' She patted Oscar's kicking foot, deluding herself a bit longer.

She needed a strong drink but she couldn't have one so Tim Tams would have to do. Hauling herself off of the couch, she waddled through the now dark house into the kitchen. Moonlight filtered through the window while she filled the kettle, the darkness unable to dent the late summer heat that hung torpidly over everything. As she flicked off the tap, the outside sensor lamp burst into light, illuminating the back entrance.

'Hey, BJ, are you hungry?' Tess glanced at the cat door, expecting Carolyn's stately black and white cat to step through and give her his usual disdainful look.

The flap stayed perfectly still.

The scrape of a key in the lock sent a prickle of alarm scudding through her. No one else had a key. Who could possibly be coming into the house? With her heart pounding hard against her ribs, she reached for the knife block with one hand and the phone with the other.

The back door partially opened and with an indignant miaow the cat shot into the kitchen as if he'd been stepped on.

'Bloody cat.' A deep voice sounded against the clatter of keys hitting the concrete step.

Tess stifled a scream and immediately dropped the

phone. Grabbing the torch from the bench, she pressed down the black switch and swung it wildly toward the door.

'Don't take another step!' Tess's voice sounded far more in control than she felt.

The door opened fully, revealing a tall man whose broad shoulders nearly filled the doorway. He immediately put his hand up to his forehead, shielding his eyes from the brilliant light of the torch. His other hand groped the architrave, his long, lean fingers finding and pressing the white plastic light switch as if he had prior knowledge of the house. Light flooded the kitchen.

'I'm sorry. I didn't mean to startle you.'

His baritone voice rolled around her, smooth and soothing, like Swiss chocolate melting on her tongue. 'Haven't you heard of a doorbell?' Tess's hand shook and the torchlight bounced around, now overcome by the main light.

His lips formed a tight smile, exhaustion lining the deep brackets around his mouth. 'I assumed the house was empty.'

Piercing grey eyes ringed with thick, long lashes caught her gaze, sending a wave of unexpected heat thudding through her. Her heart jumped into her throat as confusion clawed at her, and her brain shot into overdrive, trying to make sense of it all. Surely the real-estate agents weren't dealing with the estate already? And if he was an agent, he wasn't from Narranbool because she knew Collin Smithon well. Yet there was an air of familiarity about him.

She pulled herself up to her full height of five feet eleven and tried to look imposing and in command despite being eight and a half months pregnant. Dusting off her imperious doctor's voice, which she hadn't used in a long time, she straightened her shoulders. 'Who are you and why do you have a key?'

He tilted his head to the side, the light picking up streaks of silver in his jet-black hair. His high cheekbones carried the gauntness of fatigue and black stubble lined his strong jaw, giving him a renegade look. For the second time in as many minutes his gaze zeroed in on her as if he was seeing past her face and down into her essence, the place she kept hidden away. Goosebumps tangoed with sweat as hot and cold simultaneously raced through her.

He didn't move from the doorway but his innate aura of command radiated through his posture and his voice. 'I'm Callum Halroyd. Who are you and why are you in my brother's house?'

Tess stared in disbelief at the man she'd heard scant mention of and had never met. Blood rushed from her head as her last window of make-believe vanished before her eyes. Tomorrow had just arrived.

Cal gazed at the heavily pregnant woman in front of him and watched the blood drain from her elfin face. Hell, he'd scared the living daylights out of her. Striding into the kitchen, he pulled out a chair. 'Perhaps you should sit down.'

The woman stayed where she was, swaying slightly, her hand curled tightly around the turn of the bench.

Damn it, the last thing he needed after a twenty-four-hour flight, ninety minutes in a helicopter and a heart-breaking time with his aging and grief-stricken parents, was a pregnant woman fainting on him. He

moved slowly toward her, his palms open in a concil-
iatory gesture. 'Please, you really do need to sit down.'
He gently put his hand over hers, planning to release her
fingers so he could guide her into the chair.

An unexpected blast of heat burst through him as his
palm connected with the back of her hand. That was
strange and unexpected. Jet-lag and grief had obviously
affected his body's thermostat.

She quickly pulled her hand out from under his.
'Thanks, I'll be fine once I sit down.'

As she turned toward the proffered chair, strands of
short honey-blonde hair swept across his cheek, trailing
a scent of fresh coconut and tropical fruits. He had the
craziest desire to close his eyes and breathe in deeply
to banish the scent of war and pain that had taken up
residence without him realising it.

He gave himself a shake and quickly filled a glass
with water.

She spoke softly. 'So you're James's brother?'

'Yes, I think we established that.' He offered the
glass to the unknown woman. 'And you are…?'

She accepted the glass with her left hand and he
realised she wasn't wearing a wedding ring. Still,
pregnant women often had to remove their rings due to
fluid accumulation so that meant very little.

Wide brown eyes appraised him while she slowly
sipped her water, the action disconcerting him. He
wasn't used to being kept waiting. He was a surgeon—
he called the shots and everyone else jumped.

She lowered her glass and placed it on the bench,
before reaching out and touching his arm. 'I'm so very
sorry for your loss.'

My loss. He rubbed his forehead, rubbing the ache that had permanently throbbed since he'd heard the news.

'James and Carolyn were my dearest friends and I've been staying with them for a few months while…' She blinked rapidly.

He stifled a sigh. Typical James. He took in waifs and strays and Carolyn actively encouraged him. Now, as well as sorting out the estate, he had a pregnant, homeless woman on his hands. Yet another thing for him to organise as there was no way his parents were up to it.

He'd hardly recognised them at the airport. It was like they'd had the stuffing knocked out of them. Normally sheer energy and drive radiated from both of them, the characteristics that had made them millions from self-storage. But his usually in-control father had deferred every decision to Cal and his mother had just sat stoically silent, holding her husband's hand.

He cleared his throat. 'What about a cup of tea? God knows, I need one.'

A quiet smile stole across her heart-shaped face. 'Thank you, that would be lovely. White, no sugar, please. The tea's in the canister by the kettle.'

'And I remember that three years ago the cups were kept in the cupboard over the sink.'

She nodded. 'They're still there.'

He plugged in the kettle and spied the partially opened Tim Tams. He smiled at the memory of the luscious chocolate biscuit that his mother would allow to celebrate gold stars on homework. 'I haven't had a Tim Tam in years.'

She arched her eyebrows in mock horror. 'Why on earth not? They're the panacea for all ills.'

He heard himself laugh and a kernel of feeling other than sorrow opened up inside him. 'I haven't been living in places where supermarkets stock them. Actually, I haven't been living in places with supermarkets, full stop.' The kettle shut off and he poured the boiling water over the fragrant leaves.

'Where have you come from?'

He caught her gaze on his rumpled clothes. 'Africa.'

She smiled, her eyes taking on the warm hues of polished oak. 'James said you were busy saving the world.'

His hand tightened on the handle of the teapot as he poured the aromatic brew into fine, white cups, her words bringing back the last fraught conversation he and James had shared over three years ago. He didn't want to think about that. Not now.

'Well, I don't know about saving the world but I work for Frontline Aid. I go where I'm needed.'

'And now you're needed here.' She ran her hand over her swollen belly, in a caress than radiated love.

A sense of unease that he couldn't explain burrowed into him, pushing deep. 'I'm just here for the funeral and to help execute the will, although one of Dad's company lawyers can handle most of it. That's why I left Mum and Dad at the motel and came over to the house tonight. I need to find James's will and get the ball rolling.' He placed her steaming cup on the bench next to her.

She bit her lip, as her high forehead creased in thought. 'So once you've seen to that, you'll leave? What about your parents?'

He frowned, not liking her accusatory tone. She surely had enough to worry about with her own situation without judging him. 'I'll certainly spend some time with my parents but they understand my work is overseas.'

She traced the handle of her cup with her forefinger. 'So there's nothing to keep you here?'

'In Narranbool?' He laughed, unable to hide his derision. 'Not bloody likely.' Narranbool with its heat, dust and shrivelled wheat crops had been James's choice—one he himself had never understood.

Her shoulders stiffened and her chin tilted up as she shot him a look that reminded him so much of James and Carolyn that she could have been channelling them.

Contrition niggled at him and he sighed. 'Look, I'm sorry, but small country towns and I are not a match. In fact, Australia and I are no longer a match, and I'm not sure we ever really were. For as long as I can remember I've looked beyond this "wide brown land", I'm an ex-pat through and through.'

She nodded slowly and then grazed her plump bottom lip with her top teeth.

Try as he may to pull his gaze away, it stayed riveted on the moist lushness. What would those rosy lips taste like?

The random thought shocked him. It was official—exhaustion had made him lose control of all common sense. He was a world-renowned trauma surgeon. He didn't lust after homeless, pregnant women.

She sipped her tea, her expression thoughtful. 'What if you had a nephew—would you stay then?'

Surely her child wasn't James's? He immediately

shook away the uncharitable thought. His brother had loved his wife dearly, so much, in fact, that he'd given up plenty to be with her. No, this woman in front of him was pregnant by someone else, homeless and distraught from the shock of losing her philanthropists, which was why she was making no sense at all.

He leaned forward, talking slowly as if he was explaining complicated surgery in layman's terms. 'James and Carolyn couldn't have and didn't have any children. Now, as my twin and only sibling is dead, the chances of me being an uncle are impossible.'

She folded her hands on top of her belly and calm serenity washed over her. 'James and Carolyn have a child.'

His head pounded. The urge to dismiss her words as irrational ramblings couldn't still the disquiet, which grew like a tumour pressing on his chest. 'That's impossible. I would have known, he would have told me, my parents would have told me.'

She sat in front of him completely unruffled. 'They don't know yet. I was going to tell them tomorrow when I met them.'

Her quiet yet determined words blasted into him as the floor seemed to fall away from under his feet and the world tilted despite him being seated. He struggled to make sense of it all. 'Who are you really?'

'I'm Dr Tess Dalton, the surrogate mother of James's and Carolyn's son.'

CHAPTER TWO

A SURROGATE.

Cal stood up, needing to move, needing to pace, needing to do something. His rampaging thoughts battered his already overloaded brain, which struggled to absorb the astonishing news. *A child*.

An apologetic expression passed over Tess's face. 'I'm sorry to totally stun you like that but there's no shockproof way of delivering the news.' She hauled herself out of the chair and picked up the packet of Tim Tams. 'Here, take them all. You look like you need them more than I do.'

Caught in her understanding gaze, he distractedly bit into a biscuit. It tasted like cardboard, his body unable to experience anything other than shock. He was going to be an uncle.

The uncle of an orphan. The realisation thundered through him as he spun away from her and continued pacing. He suddenly stopped and swung back, taking a really close look at Tess. Her honey smooth skin shone with lustrous good health and her egg-blue singlet curved over voluptuous breasts. Heated blood shot through him, straight to his groin.

Stunned by his reaction, he pulled his gaze to her belly, forcing the doctor in him to appraise the pregnancy, which she carried low.

Primigravidas may experience lightening and engagement at thirty-six weeks. The information he'd absorbed long ago when he'd been a medical student pushed up from the recesses of his mind and forced down the unwanted lust. 'Exactly when *is* the baby due?'

She brushed back her fringe. 'I'm thirty-seven weeks.'

'So you're due any day.' He couldn't stop the rising inflection of his voice as an edge of panic tightened his chest.

She smiled her quiet, serene smile. 'Or in three weeks' time, yes.'

He ran his hand frantically through his hair as if that would help him make sense of it all. Yesterday his world had been familiar. Today it was as if he'd landed on an alien planet.

Unspoken thoughts tumbled from his mouth. 'But I don't understand. Why didn't we know?'

You hadn't spoken to your brother in three years, since you accused him of throwing away his life. He ignored the voice of reason. 'James could have at least told our parents. Hell, they live in the same country.'

Sympathy wove across her cheeks. 'James and Carolyn wanted your parents to meet, hold and love Oscar before—'

He started. 'Is that the child's name?' It triggered a faint memory from his childhood—the imaginary friend he and James had created to solve disputes between them.

'Yes. Oscar Callum.'

Guilt ripped at Callum and he tried to shrug it off. 'You were saying they wanted mum and dad to meet him before what?'

She sucked in her cheeks. 'Before they learned of his unorthodox birth.' Her gaze dropped away. 'Before the press got wind of it.'

The money. Dad's money. It was an inescapable fact that the Halroyd millions often generated intense media interest and it was no secret that James had taken a low profile to avoid media intrusion in his life. He stared at the woman in front of him, struck by a sudden thought. 'Is there money involved?'

Her chin tilted up sharply. 'It's exactly that attitude which made Carolyn and James decide to hold off telling you. Money played no part in this. I did it out of love.'

If gold sparks were daggers, her eyes would have knifed him clean through the heart. *Love.* He swallowed a groan. He didn't believe in love. His job didn't allow for it and Felicity had crushed any remaining thoughts. But now wasn't the time for a philosophical discussion about whether love existed or not.

A baby was coming into his family in the next few weeks and nothing he could do would change that. Every plan he'd made for the immediate future swirled in his mind like dust in the wind, being carried further and further away from him. He wanted to put his hand out and grab on tight to all his arrangements but there was nothing to hold onto. Everything had changed.

He sucked in a deep breath and slowly all the confusion in his mind cleared. This was no different from triage at Frontline. Decisions had to be made and priorities needed to be set. He knew immediately what he had to do.

Tess could almost see the cogs of Callum's mind working behind those enigmatic dark grey eyes. As tall as James was short and as dark as James had been fair, Callum was the physical opposite of his fraternal twin. But the differences didn't stop there.

James had never made her heart pound or her stomach somersault. He'd been her best friend's husband, a kind man, a great doctor and the brother she'd never had. She thought back to her ill-fated relationship with Curtis. Not even in their halcyon early days had she ever felt quite this weirdly agitated and tingly.

She pushed away these new sensations and focused on what she knew about Callum, which wasn't much as James had only ever mentioned him in passing. *His biological uncle isn't exactly the 'kick a footy to the kid' type of guy.*

Callum's suddenly brisk, businesslike voice broke into her thoughts. 'So you're booked into the Women's Hospital in Melbourne to have my nephew?'

The 'take-charge' doctor had replaced the bewildered man and his question surprised her. 'Ah, no, I planned to have the baby here.'

He raised his black brows. 'So Narranbool Bush Hospital has acquired a neonatal intensive care unit since I last visited.'

She ignored his sarcasm. 'Narranbool District Hospital has probably lost beds since you were last in the country. It's a constant battle to keep country hospitals open, accredited and debt free. With sixty births a year we hardly qualify for an NICU.'

He folded his arms, his eyes darkening. 'My point exactly. We need to get you down to Melbourne tomorrow as soon as the funeral is over. You can stay in the east wing of my parents' house in Toorak and then you're close to the Women's when you go into labour.'

Her blood pounded in her head as her hands started to shake. She fisted them closed to steady them against the cocktail of emotions that pounded her. Her worst fear of what Carolyn had always jokingly referred to as 'Halroyd organisation' was swinging into action faster than she'd thought possible.

She kept her voice steady against all her fears about the Halroyds taking over that had plagued her from the moment she'd learned of her friends' deaths. She was a surrogate, not family. 'I don't want to stay in the east wing.'

He frowned, momentarily nonplussed. 'I don't understand. It's independent of the rest of the house and has everything you could possibly need for your confinement. Besides, my parents wouldn't hear of you staying in a hotel and you won't be inconveniencing them at all if that's your concern.'

His determination and authoritative tone slammed into her like a truck hitting a brick wall. 'Look, it's very kind of you to offer but—'

'It's not a matter of kindness, it's the best thing to do.' His matter-of-fact voice brooked no argument.

'The best thing?' She failed to keep the incredulity out of her voice. 'I can't just up and leave Narranbool.'

'Why on earth not?' The derision in his voice matched the perplexity on his face.

Because I'm the only doctor here. But she knew

telling him that wasn't going to help her cause to stay in town and have Oscar. She'd just have to hope he would respect the wishes of his brother. She cradled her hands under her stomach. 'James and Carolyn wanted to have the baby here and I'm going to respect their wishes.'

His brow creased in confusion. 'So there's another doctor in Narranbool with obstetric qualifications?'

She skirted the question. 'I've got my diploma in obstetrics.'

The creases deepened. 'No matter how talented a doctor you are, Tess, you cannot deliver the baby.' He pressed his palms down onto the scoured wooden benchtop and leaned forward, the muscles in his arms taut with tension. 'Who is going to deliver my nephew?' His quiet words hung between them.

My nephew. His family. Oscar's family. She hesitated as if she teetered on the very tip of a steep mountain, knowing that no matter which way she moved, she would tumble and fall. Fall into his plan of going to Melbourne. She met his piercing gaze. 'The midwives are experts in healthy, straightforward labours and—'

'But James isn't here to act as back-up.' Callum's softly spoken words exposed the flaw that now made the original plan less workable if complications did arise.

For three days she'd been on the phone, following leads for another doctor with obstetric qualifications, but all conversations had ended in 'No'. But she hadn't given up hope; she still had time to find someone. Like all other outback women before her, she wanted to have her baby in her town and Oscar deserved to be born in the place his parents had adored.

She plastered what she hoped was a reassuring smile on her face. 'But I'm healthy and the baby is healthy so the chances of me needing a doctor are pretty slim. Worst case scenario, we're a short helicopter ride to Mildura which is a lot better than women in Africa—'

'But we're not in Africa, we're in Australia.' His previously warm voice had chilled to a stony determination.

'Yes, we're in Australia, and as I pointed out I have access to emergency care if it's needed. There are other pregnant women in this town, Callum, and I'm not suggesting to them that they all decamp to Melbourne.'

A flash of sorrow flared in his eyes before a muscle in his jaw twitched. 'Your job is to safeguard *my* nephew and I want you giving birth with the full suite of backup that modern medicine can offer on the other side of the double doors.'

She stared at his implacable stance, his mouth set in a firm line and his arms crossed over his broad chest. Knowing that exhaustion, grief and pain were driving him, she swallowed her biting retort that she would never put his nephew at risk either. Wearily she pushed at her fringe with her fingers and stalled. 'Let's talk about this tomorrow, after a night's sleep, after the funeral.'

'There's nothing more to talk about.'

She sighed. 'There are *so* many things to talk about.' *Like the fact that if I leave town, Narranbool has no doctor.* The unmistakeable ring of her mobile interrupted her. She glanced at the display. 'Excuse me, I have to take this call.' She punched the green button. 'Tess Dalton speaking.'

She listened carefully as Rosie Whitherton, the director of nursing at the hospital, told her that a patient had arrived and needed to see her.

'I'll be right there.' She snapped her phone shut, relief surging through her that work would definitely end this conversation with Callum. 'I'm sorry, but I have to go.' She hunted around for her car keys, which always sank into the furthest corner of her voluminous tote bag.

'Go where?' His body rippled with alertness as if a 'go' button had just been pushed, locking down all his previous emotions.

'To work.' Her fingers touched every possible handbag item except the cool metal of keys. 'There's an emergency at the hospital.'

'You're on call?' Surprise spun along his cheeks, vanishing almost as quickly as it had arrived.

She held her breath, hoping it was a rhetorical question, wanting to keep her cover until the last possible moment.

He shrugged and picked up his keys. 'I'll come with you.'

Astonishment flipped her stomach. She needed a break from this conversation and she didn't need Callum Halroyd with his intense stare and his questioning and organising demeanour entering her professional domain. He disconcerted her enough in the kitchen, let alone in A and E.

She started lifting newspapers, still searching for her keys. 'But you're exhausted. Shouldn't you get some sleep?'

He exhaled a ragged breath and hooked her gaze. 'Have you slept since you heard the news?'

She bit her lip and shook her head. 'Point taken.' He needed work as much as she did right now and she couldn't insist that he stay behind.

Abandoning her key hunt completely, she swung her bag over her shoulder and strode purposefully to the door as much as a pregnant woman could stride. As her hand grasped the doorknob she turned back toward Callum, catching his resolute expression, which contrasted starkly with an unexpected glint in his dark eyes.

Excitement? She suddenly saw him in a different light. Instead of grief being front and centre, an overlay of anticipation shimmered around him. Was Callum an adrenaline junkie? A doctor who worked in war zones as much for himself as for patients. Did work excite him? The thought coiled through her, settling in the back of her mind to be re-examined later.

'Let's go.' She stepped into the hot night, half dreading and half looking forward to working with this enigmatic man.

And that scared the hell out of her.

Callum assessed the small emergency department of Narranbool District Hospital through the glass panel of the door and sighed. How had James stood working in this two-horse town? The equipment looked older than some of the gear he used in Africa.

Rosie, the DON, had greeted him and Tess with open arms and an apologetic grimace, and had immediately disappeared back to the nursing home to check on a patient. Typical country medicine—under-resourced, understaffed and underwhelming. Bush hospitals had become glorified nursing homes as mainstream surgical procedures were removed to the capital cities and larger regional centres, which had all the up-to-date equipment.

The trip to the hospital had been quick and silent, with the exception of Tess's husky voice giving navigating instructions. To shut out lust, Callum had made lists in his head of the things he had to organise, including pulling in a favour from a mate who was an obstetrician in Melbourne. The sooner Tess was in Melbourne the better.

Then he could relax.

He ignored the faint voice in his head that he was overreacting, that Tess was right about the safety of giving birth in Narranbool and that he was medicalising childbirth. James was dead and nothing he could do would change that. But he could do everything possible to safeguard James's son.

He rubbed his temples with his thumb and forefinger. And there was still the problem of his parents. He had no idea how to gently tell two shocked sixty-five-year-olds that they were soon to be grandparents.

Tess grabbed a couple of gowns off the linen trolley, the soft fabaric of her shorts tightening on her behind.

His gaze fixed itself on the plump roundness, his mind immediately imagining how his hands would feel curved against the softness. *You're gawking at a pregnant woman. Now, that's really classy.*

Tess turned, the expression in her chocolate eyes quizzical as she tossed him a gown. 'Here—catch.'

Her words brought him instantly back to the A and E. Abandoning his lustful thoughts, he immediately became the doctor. 'What do we know about this patient?'

Tess picked up the beige history folder with the distinctive colour-coded spine that was used in most hospitals around the country. 'Rosie said he's a relative of a local family, visiting from Perth. He hasn't been feeling well since dinner and has complained of heartburn.'

'That's the emergency?' He tugged on his gown and sighed. 'He probably just needs some antacid and a lecture on the evils of overeating.'

'You were the one who wanted to come to the hospital.' She gave him an arch look. 'We could wish him a myocardial infarction if that's more exciting for you.'

Her barb hit with unerring accuracy. He loved the rush of an emergency, of dealing with the unknown, having to think on his feet and being just one step ahead of disaster. 'Sorry. GP work just isn't me.'

'No? Really? I would never have guessed.' Her wide mouth curved up into a smile that raced directly to her eyes, giving her a teasing, sassy look. 'But you're here now, action man, so follow me and watch and learn how to talk to a patient who is actually awake.'

Action man. A delicious sensation of warmth unexpectedly scudded through him. His staff at Frontline were fabulous but in Theatre he was the boss and no one ever questioned him. No one ever teased him.

As she walked away from him, an involuntary sound erupted from his throat which he recognised as laughter. A flare of something akin to happiness lightened his chest for a moment before shrinking but not completely fading. He followed her through the double doors toward the source of noise.

'You need to wait in the waiting area and we will call you back when he's seen the doctor.' A tired voice sounded over the clamour of many talking at once.

'But he's my brother.' A woman's voice rose in agitation, while her pudgy hands gesticulated, sending her many bracelets jangling.

Relatives. They were another reason why he'd become a surgeon. By the time he got to speak to relatives, other staff had usually calmed them down, and after he'd spoken to them briefly, his registrar followed up, answering any other questions.

Callum recognised the distinctive white and blue uniform of a nurse who turned toward them at the sound of the door, relief clear on her face.

'Tess, I've done baseline observations on Mr Renaldo and he's pretty uncomfortable with epigastric pain.'

'Thanks, Esther. Mr Halroyd and I will sort him out.'

The middle-aged woman nodded slowly as she took a head-to-toe look at Callum, interest and curiosity bold in her eyes. She turned back to the relatives. 'The doctors are here now and everyone needs to leave.' She pointed to the door and started herding the crowd back to the waiting area affectionately known as chairs.

Tess winked at him. 'Within the hour all of Narranbool will know you're here. Esther is a great nurse and a great communicator.'

His jaw tightened at the accepted small-town culture. 'Hmm, that sounds like code for gossip. It probably comes from not having enough to do.'

Tess frowned, her mouth opening slightly before

closing into a thin line. With a slight roll of her shoulders she walked into the examination room.

'Mr Renaldo, I'm Tess Dalton and this is Mr Callum Halroyd. He's visiting Narranbool, just like you are.' Tess gave a welcoming smile to their patient.

The pale man propped up on white pillows mustered a smile as the ECG monitor he was connected to beeped reassuringly. 'Call me Vince.'

Callum nodded in acknowledgement of the greeting.

'So what's brought you in, Vince?' Tess rested the chart board on top of her bump.

'My sister's cooking!' He gave a wry smile. 'To be fair, I haven't felt that great since I arrived and tonight the heartburn just got to me.'

Tess's face expressed sympathy as she rubbed her sternum. 'I know what you mean. I'm looking forward to eating a curry without revisiting it all night.'

Callum's patience strained to the breaking point. Small talk had never been his thing which was yet another reason why he'd chosen surgery. By now he would have asked for specific symptoms and be moving into the examination. James had been the member of the family who'd enjoyed a chat, not him.

Tess continued. 'Is the heartburn just after meals?'

Vince shook his head. 'It's been pretty constant and I haven't been eating much lately. Haven't really felt like it.'

'What's different about today that made you come to hospital?' Tess rubbed her back.

Callum caught the action and wondered again why she was still on the on-call roster. Surely the registrar could have taken this case.

Vince grimaced and spoke between quick breaths. 'Today's a lot worse. I feel really crook, like I'm going to hurl, and I've got gut-ache too.' He gripped the bowl Esther had given him, his knuckles white against the metal.

'Have you vomited today?'

Beads of sweat formed on his forehead. 'No, but I've had some diarrhoea and I dunno what my sister cooked but it was as black as tar!'

Tess immediately glanced over their patient's head and caught Callum's gaze, her brown eyes full of concern. Black bowel motions meant blood.

Callum reached for the stethoscope that hung over the top of the BP machine, planning to hand it to Tess.

'Vince, we need to examine you and I'm going to ask Callum to do that while I insert an intravenous drip into your arm. When the nurse took your temperature it was up, and it's always good to have some extra fluids on board when you have a fever.'

And when there's a possibility that you're bleeding internally. Tess knew her stuff and had swung into a team action approach. He couldn't fault her decision and the thrill of excitement he got from work kicked in.

'If you can lie down for me, I'll palpate your abdomen.' Callum put the stethoscope around his neck.

Vince's expression became confused. 'Do what?'

Tess raised her brows at Callum, a dimple appearing briefly in one cheek. Almost as quickly the muscles in her face schooled themselves into impassivity and she looked directly at Mr Renaldo. 'He's going to gently press your stomach to see if it's tender.'

The patient's brow immediately cleared. 'Oh, right.'

He turned to Callum. 'You should have said so, Doc.'
He gingerly shuffled down the bed and lifted the gown.
'At least in this heat your hands will be warm.'

Callum silently groaned; sleeping patients didn't
give cheek. He scanned the patient's abdomen, immediately noticing it was bloated. 'Let me know if any of
this hurts.' His fingeres pressed firmly but gently,
moving over the area, seeking guarding and rigidity, and
then he examined the upper midline.

Callum pressed close to the upper midline.

Vince hissed. 'Hell, Doc, that hurts.' He pressed his
fist to his epigastric area.

'Sorry.' Callum helped him sit up to relieve the reflux
pain and then wrapped the blood-pressure cuff around
the man's upper arm. 'Are you on any medications?'

'Me knees are arthritic so I take some painkillers for
that.'

Tess swabbed Vince's left arm. 'What sort of painkillers?'

'Aspirin mostly or that new stuff with the funny
name I.-B.-something.'

The story was coming together. 'Ibuprofen.' Callum
pumped up the BP cuff.

Callum heard the swish and thud of blood in the
arteries as he released the air from the cuff and matched
the sounds to the fall of the arrow. He decided to leave
the cuff in place, wanting to monitor Vince's blood
pressure closely.

'Your BP is 110 on 75, which is a bit low. Do you
know what your usual blood press—'

Vince suddenly heaved, his eyes wide with alarm as
bright red blood filled the basin. The ECG machine
screamed a high-pitched warning sound.

Esther came running into the room, quickly taking in the emergency. She deftly removed the bowl. 'I'll measure this for blood loss.'

'Tess, is that IV in yet?' Callum quickly dropped the back of the bed down so their patient was lying flat and strapped a clear oxygen mask onto his face. For the first time since arriving at the hospital Callum relaxed. Emergencies were what he did best.

'I've got Hartmann's solution going in full bore.' Tess taped the drip into place, her expression grave. 'It looks like he just dropped a litre of blood.'

Callum gave a grim nod. 'It fits in with all the classic signs of a bleeding ulcer probably exacerbated by using non-steroidal anti-inflammatories for his arthritis.'

She placed her hand on their patient's wrist, checking his pulse. 'Vince, you're bleeding somewhere in your gut. We're replacing the blood with an electrolyte solution but we'll need to evacuate you to Mildura Base Hospital for a procedure to stop the bleeding.'

The pallid and sweaty man barely nodded his understanding.

Callum's brain went into overdrive. Vince was in no fit state for evacuation and unless they could keep his circulating volume up, he could go into cardiac arrest. He walked around to Tess, his hand gently closing around her forearm, her skin warm and soft on his palm. Guiding her a few steps aside, he spoke sotto voce. 'I don't suppose there's any chance that Narranbool Bush Hospital runs to an operating theatre and gastroscope?'

Tess bristled. 'We have visiting specialists come through here on rotation from Mildura and, yes, we do have a 'scope but no one qualified to use...' Her eyes sparkled as realisation dawned. 'You can do the scope and clip the ulcer. That's fantastic—you're just what we need.'

Her appreciation wound through him, spreading into every cell with a zing of something he didn't recognise. He grinned like a fool, which was crazy as he was only going to do something he was very qualified to do and did on a regular basis. 'I can, if you can do the anaesthetic.'

She beamed. 'That I can do.' As she started to turn back to their patient she stopped abruptly and immediately put her hand on her lower ribs.

Callum stilled. 'Something wrong?' He had this growing premonition that the baby was in danger. It was irrational, unfounded and absurd, but it bothered him that she was still working.

She laughed. 'No, just Oscar's foot doing some break dancing.' She turned back to their patient. 'Mr Renaldo, I have good news. Callum can operate on you here in Narranbool. Esther will get you ready for Theatre and I'll organise all the paperwork.'

'Whatever you have to do, Doc.' Vince's voice trembled with anxiety. 'Can you tell my sister?'

'Absolutely.' Tess squeezed Vince's hand.

Relief rolled through Callum. Tess would deal with the hysterical relatives, which suited him just fine.

'Right, let's get moving.' Completely in his element, he took charge. Grabbing the chart, he scrawled down a drug dose. 'Esther, take blood for cross-matching.'

'Right you are, Mr Halroyd.' Esther's face shone with sympathy. 'Your brother was a great doctor and Narranbool is very fortunate to have you on board now James has gone.'

No way am I 'on board'. The words rose to his mouth but he stopped them from tripping off his lips. Now wasn't the time to say that country life and country medicine were an anathema to him. They had a sick patient who needed his bleeding ulcer clipped.

Giving Esther a curt nod of appreciation, he turned to Tess, whose expression was unexpectedly calculating. But he didn't have time to wonder about that—the clock was ticking, and his adrenaline was pumping. He clapped his hands together. 'Let's get this man to Theatre now, before he bleeds any more.'

CHAPTER THREE

'I KNOW you wanted to get in fast so I've sedated him with midazolam and propofol and he's all set to go.' Tess's worried eyes looked at Callum over her theatre mask. 'He's lucky you're here.'

A niggle of concern pulled at Cal but the beeping of the monitor registering Vince's low blood pressure intervened. 'Let's start.' He put his gloved hand out for the gastroscope.

Ken Liu, the theatre nurse, handed him the long, black, flexible tube, whose plain colour belied its ability to light and electronically magnify the gut.

Cal had to give the staff credit—they'd mobilised quickly and there'd been no messing around. He glanced up at the screen as he passed the tube down the oesophagus. 'No sign of varices, always good.'

'Excellent news.' Tess's hidden smile played through her voice. 'Often patients aren't one hundred per cent honest about their history if alcohol is involved.' The ECG monitor beeped rhythmically and reassuringly next to her. 'Esther, is the blood here?'

'It's on its way but we've got plasma expander. Do

you want that put up?' Esther's questioning brows rose over her green surgical mask.

Tess checked Vince's BP. 'Right now his pressure's holding so I think we can wait for the blood.'

Cal grunted in frustration. 'His stomach's full of blood. Sucker, quickly.' He needed to clear the area and find the source of the bleeding.

Ken handed him the instrument and the sound of suction filled the tense air of Theatre. Just as suddenly it stopped. 'Damn it, the sucker's blocked by clots. Saline. I need saline to clear it.'

'Pressure's falling,' Tess stated in words what the incessant beeping told them.

He swore softly under his breath. 'I'm scubadiving here and I can't see anything except blood.' He readjusted the sucker, his hand gripping tightly, and pressed his eye hard against the viewfinder of the 'scope. *Don't bleed out on me before I find the cause.*

'The blood's arrived.' Esther called out in relief as she accepted the welcome units from the blood-bank technician.

Tess moved fast. 'Esther! Start squeezing one unit of blood into the left IV, now.' She quickly snatched the second unit out of the nurse's hands and attached it to the other large-bore IV she'd inserted.

Four hands worked furiously, pushing life saving blood into their patient, giving his heart the much-needed volume to pump around. A frown line appeared on the bridge of Tess's nose. 'Callum, how much of this is going straight into his gut?'

'More than we want.' His terse voice carried his apprehension.

'I should have tubed him.' Tess's usually calm voice sounded ragged at the edges.

He couldn't look up but he wanted to reassure her. 'You made the right choice at the time. You're not an anaesthetist and light sedation is usually better.' Tension strained every muscle as Callum moved the 'scope to find the bleeder. 'He's hosing blood, damn it, but from where?'

The sedated Vince suddenly shuddered and blood and clots projected from his mouth, all over the floor and onto Callum's shoes. He moved his feet. 'At least now I can see a bit better. No sign of a peptic ulcer.'

'I should tube him—he could aspirate.' Tess ran a fine nasal suction tube down into Vince's trachea.

Vince's half-empty stomach immediately filled with blood as Callum probed into the duodenum, the sucker working overtime. Suddenly he caught sight of inflammation, the ugly ragged edges of an ulcer with an enormous clot in the centre. *Thank you.* 'Found it. It's an enormous duodenal ulcer. No wonder he's been bleeding like a stuck pig.'

He injected the saline down the three-millimetre channel in the 'scope and sent up a prayer that it wouldn't make things worse.

Ken's eyes were glued to the screen, his voice disbelieving. 'Is that a spurting artery at the base of the ulcer?'

It had made things worse. 'Hell, yes.' The clot had been trying to seal the bleeding. He sent down more saline to clear the area of blood so he could see what needed haemotosis.

Ken immediately passed him adrenaline. 'Or will you use diathermy?'

'Adrenaline first.' His concentration brought conversation down to the bare minimum. He injected the adrenaline, wishing it speed in constricting the blood vessels and bringing the bleeding under control.

Bringing the whole situation under control. He relaxed slightly. 'Right, I'll just put the—'

The monitor screamed and Tess picked up her laryngoscope. 'His O$_2$ sats are dropping, and he's got a lung full of blood. Callum, you need to pull out now so I can tube him.'

Sweat pooled on his forehead. He was so close. 'Give me a minute to put on the haemoclip. I'm almost done.'

'We don't have a minute.' Her eyes flashed with fear and steely determination.

'Yes, we do. I've done this before.' Callum put out his hand. 'Kenny, the clip.'

The nurse hesitated, glancing between them.

'Now,' Cal barked, and the clip hit his hand.

Tess increased the nasal oxygen, her voice stern with dread. 'We're risking him arresting.'

'Trust me, I'm on it.' Callum blocked out the panic in Tess's eyes, blocked out the screaming monitors, the stunned gazes of the nursing staff and did what he did best. With the finesse of the finest craftsman he sealed the bleeding ulcer with the clip.

Exhilaration thundered through him at the save, the buzz making him feel alive in a way no other event or situation ever could. 'I'm done. The bleeder is plugged and he's all yours.' He removed the 'scope from Vince's gut.

'Thank you.' Tess smiled at him with open admiration tinged with school marm disapproval. She immediately busied herself, aspirating the blood Vince had inhaled into his lungs. 'You've done a fabulous job despite giving us all heart failure there for a minute.' Her eyes held slight censure. 'Just one more thing. You need to explain it all to Vince's sister.'

His gut dropped. James had been the 'touchy-feely' Halroyd, the people person. Cal didn't want to have to deal with hysterical relatives, especially when he knew Tess would do it so much better. 'I can wait for you and we can do it together.'

She shook her head. 'I'm going to be tied up here for a bit longer getting him stable. The family will be stressing and you need to put them out of their misery.' Her face was hidden behind her mask but her eyes said it all. 'I'll be there as soon as I can.' She turned back to Esther and issued instructions about commencing antibiotics.

Stunned, he stared at the back of her head. It wasn't supposed to work like this. He did the life-on-the-edge stuff, not the routine hack work. But Callum Halroyd, the feted Frontline surgeon, had clearly just been organised and dismissed by a country GP.

He didn't like it at all.

Callum ran his hand through his hair. Clipping the ulcer had been a walk in the park compared with the conversation he'd just endured with Vince's sister. Tess had eventually rescued him from the emotional woman and ushered him into the tiny lounge off Theatre.

Glancing over the top of his cup of steaming coffee, he noticed black smudges under Tess's eyes, marring her clear skin. She pressed one hand to the small of her back while she sipped her tea. She really should be tucked up in bed.

An image of her face relaxed in sleep and her lush body sprawled across a bed thudded through him. Despite fatigue, despite his grief, his groin tightened. *Hell.* He downed his coffee, almost welcoming the quick scald against his mouth and throat.

'Sorry about your shoes.' Tess's apologetic gaze dropped to his bare feet. 'I've never seen anyone bleed like that before, not even during my residency in Sydney.'

He gave a wry grin. 'Oh, they can bleed all right. So now you know that you always tube anyone with a belly full of blood and save the surgeon's shoes.'

'Not to mention the patient's life.' Chuckling softly, she lifted her legs up onto a chair and rotated her ankles. 'You did brilliantly tonight, action man. Thank you very much. We'd have been in strife without you, and on the plus side you got a bit of excitement tonight after all, so it was a win-win situation all round.' She smiled smugly.

He knew he'd pushed her out of her comfort zone back in Theatre. 'Sorry it got a bit hairy in there and that I *overrode* you, but I *knew* I could get the clip on.'

She shot him a knowing look. 'See, general practice isn't as mind-numbing as you seem to think.'

He snorted, unable to help himself. 'And the last time you had to open Theatre for an emergency was?'

She had the grace to look like a kid caught with her hand in the lolly jar. 'We do small procedures here and elective surgery cases go to Mildura or Wagga.'

He nodded, happy in the knowledge that he had Narranbool pegged. 'And really serious cases would go to Melbourne to state-of-the-art equipment and experienced staff. It's how the system works.' He stood up, rinsed his cup and placed it on the drainer. 'It's midnight. I'll take you home.'

Her brows pulled together as she swung her feet down onto the floor. 'I should stay a bit longer.'

'Vince is stable and in good hands with Esther and Ken. They've got my mobile number and if his condition deteriorates they'll ring. I'll visit him in the morning before the service, and check the results for *Helicobacter pylori*. I imagine that's the culprit causing the ulcer, and if so I'll start him on combined antibiotics.'

He gently took her empty cup from her hands. 'So now all you have to do is go home and crash.'

Luminous eyes stared up at him, clear and penetrating. He expected her to object, and decided to pre-empt her and not wait for the words of refusal to pour from her amazing mouth. A mouth that could go from a pout to a wide smile in a heartbeat. 'Tomorrow is going to be a long day and—'

'That sounds like a good idea.'

Amazement rocked him. 'Pardon?'

She smiled against a closed mouth, her lips compressing and her chest rocking as she stifled laughter. 'You're right. I'm exhausted and tomorrow will be huge.'

Relief trickled through him. Earlier this evening when they'd discussed going to Melbourne, he'd decided that Tess had a stubborn streak that ran long and deep. He hadn't expected her to readily agree with him about taking over Vince's care. She'd obviously come around on all fronts.

'So we're in agreement—excellent.' He quickly calculated their estimated time of departure. 'I'll pick you up at ten-thirty in the morning. I think it's best to wait until after the funeral to tell my parents—they sure don't need that sort of distraction before the service.' He shoved his hands deep in his pockets. 'There'll be hours in the car on the way to Melbourne to discuss everything and sort out the details.'

Her jaw tilted slightly and her shoulders straightened. 'I'll go to Melbourne on one condition.'

His hand automatically rubbed his forehead as he rested his bottom on the table and looked down at her. 'And what would that be?' The words rolled out on a sigh.

'That you stay here and work in Narranbool.'

He heard the words but his brain refused to believe them. 'That's a ridiculous request. Narranbool doesn't need me as part of its medical personnel.'

'*Yes*, it does.' Her sombre tone hung between them.

The serious light in her eyes, along with the tension clinging to her face, sent unease swirling through him. Slowly, through the fog that was his mind, realization dawned.

He absently rubbed the palm of his left hand with his right thumb. Tess was thirty-seven weeks pregnant and on call. There had been no reference by any of the staff of a registrar. *Narranbool is very fortunate to have you on board now James has gone*. He closed his eyes against the truth that bore down on him, hard and unyielding, like an avalanche. Forcing his eyes open, he met her gaze. Not even bothering to ask it as a question, he spoke slowly. 'You're the only doctor in town now.'

She nodded. 'That's right.'

The idea of working in a small town almost choked

him. He'd go stark raving mad being a GP, listening to a catalogue of rambling woes and ailments, but no town deserved to lose all its medical personnel in the one week. Still, he needed Tess safe in Melbourne, needed to keep the baby safe.

He dragged in a resigned breath. 'So you'll go to Melbourne if I stay here? That's blackmail.'

'No, it's not—it's a choice.' She folded her arms and even though she was sitting and he was standing, no way was she a powerless participant. 'I refuse to leave my community without medical care. If you want Oscar born in Melbourne then this is the best solution.'

Every cell in his body railed at the idea. 'What about me being in Melbourne for the birth of my nephew?'

'I have three weeks to go until my due date and we'll have organised another doctor by then.' A slow smile washed over her face as her eyes glowed with keen intelligence. 'Of course, if you can't hack the slow pace of an outback general practice, I can stay in town and keep working.'

His gut rolled as personal need clashed violently with professional ethics. He didn't want to stay in Narranbool, damn it, but he couldn't leave the town without a doctor. He rubbed the back of his neck, his fingers hardly making a dent in the tight muscles. She had him well and truly over an ethical barrel.

Trying hard to keep the growl out of his voice, he marched to the door, car keys in hand. 'There'd better be a GP here within the week.'

Tess sipped a lemon, lime and bitters, welcoming the cooling bubbles against her tongue. Ceiling fans circled slowly, moving the hot, dry air through the church hall. People milled in clusters, talking, drinking and eating the glorious spread of food that the Country Women's Association had put together.

She rolled her shoulders and leaned back, trying to increase the space between the baby and her ribs. She pressed down on Oscar's foot, which constantly pushed back, making her abdomen feel tight and strained. Her back ached, her front ached and she couldn't find a comfortable position. It had been difficult to sit in the church and she'd felt fidgety and restless, but then again who ever felt relaxed at such occasions? It had been an ordeal to say goodbye to her dearest friends.

Jennifer and Patrick, Callum's parents, moved from group to group, seeking stories and affirmations about James and Carolyn, a vital role of a funeral. Oscar's grandparents seemed frailer than she'd expected and she wondered if they were up to having her stay in their home or even dealing with a newborn baby once he arrived. She'd been steeling herself for 'the talk' on the long drive to Melbourne.

Not that she wanted to go to Melbourne, but she had no choice now she'd hammered out a deal with the devil in the guise of Callum Halroyd. How could one man with grey eyes that could darken to inky black reduce her legs to jelly with one long look? He was the most handsome and charismatic man she'd ever met.

Despite every resolve not to, Tess found herself watching Callum's movement around the hall. She kidded herself that with his height and colouring he stood out from the crowd and was hard to miss, so really she wasn't seeking him out. But she recognised the rationalisation for what it was. A complete lie. He drew her gaze all the time and, so help her, she enjoyed watching him. He commanded a room just by standing in it.

He'd tried to command her last night but she couldn't have let that happen. She needed some control in this situation when everything she'd expected about her future had suddenly changed. So she'd gambled on his sense of duty and won. At least Narranbool had a doctor, no matter how grudging, until the future was more certain.

A mild cramp above her pubic bone forced her to shift position, and she transferred her weight from one foot to the other, trying not to think about the short time she had left with Oscar. She must be the only pregnant woman on earth who wanted to go two weeks over her due date.

She dreaded his birth. Not because she was scared about labour but because she was scared about what would come afterwards. Nothing about the future had been discussed yet, but Callum's determination to get her to Melbourne spoke loudly that Oscar was a Halroyd and the Halroyds would make all the decisions about Oscar.

But he's mine, too. She bit her lip. Her role as a surrogate was to give the child up to his parents and she'd been happy with that, never giving it a second thought. Especially as she'd been seriously considering staying in Narranbool and joining James in the practice so she could be a hands-on auntie.

Now everything had changed. Carolyn and James were dead, the Halroyds would claim the child and a fax had just arrived from London, asking her when she would be starting the job she'd already delayed once.

She had no idea what her future held now or how she could be involved in the baby's life, but she knew that giving birth and giving Oscar up immediately was all too quick. She needed more time than that.

The baby kicked again and seemed to lurch sideways suddenly, as if he was doing a somersault. Immediately the muscles of her belly stiffened into rigidity, the spasm hitting with unexpected force and the sharp pain making her gasp. Her fingers tightened so hard around the glass she thought it might break.

She heard a 'pop'. She stared down at the glass but it was still intact.

Wetness suddenly trickled down her thigh, warm and sticky. *Your waters just broke.*

No, no, no!

She was just hot and it was sweat. She wasn't ready to go into labour. She wasn't ready to have Oscar. She wasn't ready to give him up to the world, give him up to the Halroyds.

Her belly relaxed as the spasm passed. Small rivulets of fluid ran down behind her knee, marking a trail of certainty. *A hind-water rupture will be a slow leak.*

It didn't matter what she wanted, the die was cast. Some time in the next twenty-four hours she would give birth to a little boy.

Oh, man, she didn't want a fuss, she wanted a quiet exit from the hall without anyone realising what had just happened. Especially Callum and the senior Halroyds. They didn't need to be rushed away from the wake. Besides, rupture of membranes without contractions usually meant the baby was in a posterior position, which translated to a long, slow, backache labour. She had hours ahead of her before things really got moving.

Thinking fast, she deliberately bumped against the table as her hand collided with a jug of cordial. Sticky lemon drink cascaded over her, spilling onto the floor, merging with amniotic fluid and disguising the faint musky-sweet odour. She jumped back as if startled. 'Oh, I'm so clumsy.'

Immediately, Millie Hendry scurried toward her, mop in hand. 'Don't worry, dear. Soon you won't have to worry about allowing for that bump.'

Sooner than you think, Millie. Tess gave a wry smile.

'The cordial is supposed to go in your mouth, not down your front,' Callum's rumbling voice teased close behind her, his breath caressing her ear.

Traitorous warmth surged again, spreading through her like warm syrup over ice cream—sweet and tempting. 'I can't believe I was so uncoordinated.'

Callum glanced around, his gaze searching for his parents before returning to her. 'I'll take you home.'

She shook her head. 'I'm fine to get home on my own.' She hadn't had a hint of a contraction since her waters had broken, just dull backache. It was all adding up to a classic first labour—long and slow. There was probably enough time for Callum to evacuate her to Melbourne via the Halroyd Enterprises helicopter.

'It's *not* an inconvenience.' Callum placed his hand under Tess's forearm, his fingers pressing slightly against the fine sheen of sweat on her skin. He guided her around the spill on the floor and toward the door.

In the short time she'd known him, she knew it was

pointless to argue once he'd made up his mind and was in 'take-charge' mode. Instead, she sneaked a look at him, noticing how his hair had fallen forward and now touched his brows. She had the urge to smooth it back. 'I'm really sorry this means you have to leave early.'

He opened the door and ushered her outside, the afternoon heat hitting like an inferno. 'No need to apologise. I was ready to go a while ago.'

'But your parents need longer.'

Grey eyes appraised her. 'Yeah. It's like they're soaking up every story this town has about James and Carolyn.'

She chewed her lip. 'It's something to hold onto.'

'Pretty soon they'll have a baby to hold onto.' He pressed the buttons to deactivate the car alarm on his father's Mercedes as his stark words hovered.

My baby. Tess swallowed hard as dread skated down her spine, emphasising how much she was about to lose. 'We need to talk about—' She stopped abruptly as Callum opened the car door for her.

Panic flared. No way could she sit down on leather seats. Amniotic fluid was murder on upholstery and when she stood up Callum would know what had happened and insist she go straight to hospital. She knew she had plenty of time to go home, put on a pad and get her bag before checking in.

She always laughed at films when a pregnant woman's waters broke and she went instantly into full-on labour. It rarely happened that way in real life. She'd already spilled cordial all over herself so what was another white lie? 'It's only a block to the house. Let's walk.'

Incredulity climbed up his cheekbones and streaked across his handsome face. 'You're kidding, right? It's got to be over thirty-seven degrees.'

'And the car will be over fifty. It's such a short distance that the car won't have time to cool down. Let's save greenhouse emissions and walk.' She stepped away from him, trying to walk normally despite sticky, wet underpants.

Frowning, he caught up with her, his long legs striding out. 'Are you OK? It's been a big few days for you.'

She stared into his face, unexpectedly full of concern, and something inside her turned over. 'And you, too.'

A long sigh shuddered out of him. 'It sounds an awful thing to say, but I'm glad it's over.'

She knew exactly what he meant and squeezed his hand, the action seeming more natural than words.

His fingers gently closed around her hand, trapping it in his as they walked in silence through the sweltering heat. It should have felt awkward, having her hand held by a man she'd known less than twenty-four hours, but instead it was strangely reassuring.

A dull ache moved across her lower abdomen and her hand tightened automatically, dragging on Callum's as she breathed in deeply.

She heard his sharp intake of breath as they reached the gate and felt his arm wrap around her waist.

'I told you it was too hot to walk.' Supporting her with one arm, he opened the heavy oak front door with the other. 'It's time you accepted that you're close to having a baby and you need to slow down.'

You don't know how close. 'Yes, Doctor.' Grateful to

be home in the refreshing coolness of the stone cottage, Tess was prepared to agree just to keep him off the track for a bit longer.

His eyes narrowed at her ready compliance. 'I've arranged for a limousine to take you and my parents back to Melbourne.'

I won't be needing it. She kept her tone flippant. 'A limo? Isn't that a bit of overkill?'

A muscle spasmed in his cheek and a flash of hurt scooted through his eyes, turning them a darker shade of grey. 'I noticed you've been uncomfortable all day and I thought you'd appreciate the extra room. It will also make conversation easier with my parents as you'll be facing each other.' The warmth in his voice had been replaced with a hint of chill.

A stab of regret pierced her. She'd just taken his good intentions and thrown them back at him, and hurt his feelings in the process.

'I'm sorry, Callum. I'm just hot and tired and sticky and…' Another dull ache ground through her, spreading from front to back. 'I'll feel better when I've had a wash and changed my clothes. Excuse me.'

Breathing in slowly, she used every ounce of energy to make herself walk normally to the bathroom. Closing the Baltic pine door behind her, she stripped off her clothes and stepped into the shower. Setting the water-saver timer to three minutes, she adjusted the flow and let lukewarm water cascade over her.

She circled a fruity soap tenderly over her stomach and spoke softly. 'How's it going in there, buddy?'

Bending down to pick up the shampoo bottle, she

suddenly stalled, totally forgetting to breathe as tightness wound through her like a coil, the pressure building in intensity. Was that a real contraction?

She blew out a breath. Perhaps things were starting. If she had another one within ten minutes she'd tell Callum, but even then there was plenty of time. She had another long night ahead of her at the hospital, except this time she'd be the patient. Quickly soaping her hair, she rinsed off, always aware of the need to conserve water.

As her hand wrenched the tap to the right, shutting off the water, a contraction hit with the force of a truck, sucking the breath from her lungs and the strength from her legs. A heaviness dragged down in her pelvis, increasing the pressure at the top of her thighs as the spasm burned through her with growing intensity. Nothing existed except twisting, burning pain.

The electronic beep of the water timer suddenly sounded around her, its incessant noise penetrating her pain-filled brain.

Three minutes.

She rested her head against the glass of the shower cubicle, breathing hard, as the contraction faded, leaving a hard pressure between her legs.

Two contractions in less than three minutes.

Oh, God, this was it. All that discomfort she'd been in all day had actually been labour and she hadn't realised it. Another contraction pulled her uterus tight, inexorably pushing Oscar down toward the outside world.

She'd run out of excuses. She'd run out of time. This baby was coming.

Not caring that she was soaking wet, not caring that she was naked, she did the last thing she'd ever expected to do or say.

Somehow she managed to move from the shower. Pulling the door open, she yelled, 'Callum, I need you—*now*!'

CHAPTER FOUR

THE urgency in Tess's voice ripped through Cal like a bullet to the heart. He dropped the cup he was holding and ran the short distance down the hall to the bathroom. 'Tess, what's wr—'

He didn't need to ask. Leaning over the clawfoot bath, a towel slipping from her smooth, honey-coloured back, Tess was panting like a marathon runner.

He gripped the doorframe, his rational mind instantly crushing the shimmer of sensation that had shot through him at the sight of all that golden skin. 'I'll get the car and take you to hospital.'

She turned toward him, her brown eyes huge in her face like a doe caught in headlights, and she gasped out, 'No…time.'

An edge of panic vibrated in his chest. 'Of course there's time. First babies don't just pop out.'

Her breathing slowed and she sagged onto her knees. 'I've had irregular twinges all day and my waters broke in the hall.'

Disbelief slugged him so hard he almost staggered. He pulled frantically at the towels stored above the bath on the rack, catching them as they tumbled down. He flicked open a bath blanket and tucked it around Tess.

'Why didn't you say something? Hell, you walked home!'

She started to tremble. 'I didn't know. I didn't have textbook contractions, just the odd twinge now and then, and...I didn't feel any worse than I've felt over the last few days.' Her gaze implored him to understand. 'It was important for everyone to be at the funeral and the wake. Your parents needed it and I didn't want to spoil that.'

Part of him understood and appreciated how she'd put his family ahead of herself, but stress took over and he voiced his other thought. 'But your job is to look after the baby.'

Her face crumpled as she let out a low moan and leaned over on all fours.

He recognised that moan. *Nothing* was going to stop this baby from arriving, and arriving soon. *Damn it*. His nephew wasn't supposed to be born in a bathroom. He was supposed to be safe in a hospital, with an obstetrician present and a paediatrician on hand. Agitation had him gripping the back of his head. He hadn't delivered a baby in years.

Adrenaline poured through him and he quickly surveyed his environment, his mind whirling. 'I need scissors and clamps. Where's your medical bag?'

'In...my...room.' She slumped as the contraction passed. 'Please be quick.'

He nodded and raced down the corridor to the room he'd used once three years ago when he'd tried to talk James out of living in Narranbool. The medical bag sat beside the cheval mirror and he grabbed it, never happier to see the red utilitarian nylon carrier with its black shoulder-strap.

He detoured by the kitchen and poured the boiled water from the kettle into a saucepan and then threw in a pair of scissors, setting the gas on low. He ran back to the bathroom.

Tess's knuckles gleamed white as she gripped the edge of the bath, supporting her squat. A long, deep grunt rolled from her lips as sweat trickled down her forehead.

Cal dropped down beside her and wiped her brow with a face washer. 'How are you going?'

She stared at him as if she was coming back from a trance. 'Toilet. Need to go.'

Like a computer presentation, his obstetric lecture notes beamed in his mind. Crowning. The baby's head was dilating the perineum.

She started to crawl but stopped as he put his hand on her shoulder. 'Tess, it's the baby's head.'

He couldn't believe this was happening so fast. He pushed towels between her legs to create a soft landing just in case, and snapped on a pair of gloves.

Another contraction hit her and her whole body pushed downward. Her half groan, half grunt ricocheted around the room, carrying the emotion of a life-changing event.

Her nails dug into his arm, her eyes frantic. 'It hurts!'

Torn between being a doctor and desperately wanting to support her, he knew he had no option but to make the hard choice. This was no different from Frontline. He couldn't hold her hand and mop her brow *and* deliver the baby at the same time. Forcing away non-essential thoughts, he zeroed in on the delivery. 'I need to see what's happening.'

'Just…get…him…out.' The words came out on a sob.

Cal nodded and placed his hands on her arms, guiding her so she was sitting with her back against the bath. This way she was supported and he could control the delivery. He placed his hand between her legs.

He'd expected to have to reach in further but his fingers met bone—a baby's scalp. His stomach lurched. This was a precipitate labour and with that came the risk of haemorrhage.

'The baby's head is sitting right here and with a few more contractions he'll be born.' He spoke slowly, needing her to listen and understand.

Tess didn't reply, her full attention focused on what her body was doing.

'I see black hair, Tess.' A flutter of excitement batted against his controlled focus.

'Thank goodness.' She rested her head against her knees, resting between contractions.

He placed his hand on her belly, feeling for tension. 'The next contraction you have, I need you to push, but when I say "Pant" you must stop pushing so I can guide this little guy's head out very carefully.'

Her head rose slowly, her voice ironic. 'How come you get the easy job?'

'Just lucky, I guess.' He smiled and shook his head, amazed that she'd found her sense of humour in the middle of giving birth in a bathroom.

'Oh-h-h, here goes.' With clamped lips Tess pushed and the circle of hair increased in size.

'That's great. Keep pushing.' He concentrated on

flexing the head so the smallest diameter could be delivered first. 'You can push harder.'

'Can't… Gone.' She sank back against the bath, panting for breath. 'How much longer?'

The head had retreated, but not very far. 'You're doing really well, sweetheart. We just need one or two big contractions.'

'Easy for you.' She groaned as she gripped her knees, determination lining her sweat-stained face. 'Argh!'

The long, sustained push made progress. 'Pant, Tess, pant.' His gloved right hand gently held the head while his other allowed for safe passage. He blinked away a trickle of sweat, wiping his forehead on his upper arm, the fine linen shirt sopping up the moisture. 'Small push, small.'

The head moved and fluid gushed. 'Stop pushing, stop!' Suddenly a forehead, two closed eyes, a button nose and a small chin appeared. His heart leaped in his chest. *Stay focused, it's not over yet.* 'His head's out and I'm checking for the cord so stay still, Tess.'

'I'm not…going…anywhere.' Her chest rose and fell quickly, dragging in recuperative breaths.

He held his breath as his fingers reached around the baby's neck, searching for pulsating loops of cord. He checked twice but thankfully he could only feel the softness of a small neck. 'There's no tangle of cord so push with your next contraction and—'

Tess groaned as her body tensed and then she pushed.

The baby moved forward and Cal carefully angled the top shoulder downwards for safe delivery and then guided the posterior shoulder out. The next moment a baby slithered into his arms.

Exhausted, Tess slumped back against the bath.

Cal held his own breath. *Is he breathing? Please, be breathing.*

He dried the infant's head gently with a towel and then rubbed, encouraging circulation and keeping him warm. He cleared the mucus from his mouth and nose so that his airway was clear.

With a furrowed brow and an expression of surprise huge black eyes stared up at Cal, as if to say, That was quick. His little chest rose and fell evenly and his skin, initially like alabaster, started to pink up, the healthy colour quickly spreading from his torso to his toes.

Ripping open the packet of small, yellow, plastic clamps, Cal closed them over the long cord, which slowly stopped pulsating. He could worry about cutting it later. He let out a breath and relief cascaded through him, immediately chased out by wonder and awe. His heart suddenly expanded—he'd just assisted this little miracle into the world. This tiny child. My *nephew*.

'Is he all right?' Tess's weary voice asked the universal question.

Cal tried to speak but the words felt trapped and he coughed to clear his throat. 'We've got a baby boy here.' He placed the baby into Tess's exhausted arms so she could snuggle the child against her chest and warm him with her body heat.

She gazed down at the little person cradled in her arms and immediately started touching the baby's fingers and toes, counting them off one by one.

'Apgar at one minute is nine. You can't ask for much more than that.' Cal grinned widely as he quickly tucked another towel around Tess and the baby, a growing need spreading through him to keep them both safe and warm.

Tess traced a light caress around the baby's face and she spoke softly, her voice barely audible. 'Hello, Oscar. Welcome to the world.'

A lump formed in the back of Cal's throat and he swallowed hard. He was used to post-emergency buzz, post-emergency frustration and even heartache, but he'd never experienced anything like this mix of emotions— jubilation and happiness, marvelling with awe. He was flying.

Tess glanced up, smiling, and immediately reached out her hand, gripping his forearm. 'Thank you *so* much for being here, for catching Oscar. I couldn't have done it without you.'

The rays of her radiant beam flowed over Cal like spring sunshine, warming him in places he hadn't known had been cold.

'I wouldn't have missed this for anything.' His words came out spontaneously, their truth catching him by surprise. Two days ago he hadn't even met Tess, he'd had no idea his nephew existed, and now he'd delivered him safely into the world. The feeling was inde-scribable.

His hand caressed Oscar's head but his eyes stayed fixed on Tess's glowing face. As a medical student he'd observed women giving birth before, he'd delivered babies in hospital, but all of those events paled into in-significance compared with what he'd just experienced. Tess with her short, tousled hair, her wide stubborn streak and her generous warmth had been totally amazing. 'You were incredible.'

A dimple appeared in her cheek. 'I was terrified.'

He laughed. 'So was I.' He settled in next to her, his left arm around her waist supporting her and the forefinger of his right hand tightly gripped by Oscar.

'But we did good.' Her shoulders rested naturally on his chest, her body heat flooding him, and her sweet, fresh scent of tangerine filling him.

Her eyes shone with an exhilaration and joy he'd never glimpsed in anyone before, but at the same time he recognised the emotions and knew them intimately as the very same that churned through him.

He wanted to share them, wanted to savour them and feel them and hold onto them, keeping them close. 'We did sensationally.'

Her mouth widened into a tranquil, all-knowing smile—a smile that silently stated what they'd just shared. A smile that drew his head down to hers as if a fine thread connected them and it was pulling him toward her.

He was powerless against its force and he didn't want to fight it. Without thought or hesitation he lowered his head and covered her lips with his.

Tess tasted salt and sweat, heat and wonder as Callum's mouth brushed against hers with a feather-like touch. A touch that brought her body instantly to life despite its exhaustion. Her blood, already bubbling with post-birth endorphins, erupted into a roiling sea of desire that dumped over her in tingling riffs, leaving her gasping for breath and completely confused.

His tongue trailed the most gentle and delicate line along her lower lip before his mouth slowly released hers, leaving behind only a slight lingering taste and a memory of delicious pressure.

As her brain recoiled in stunned surprise, the warm air quickly dried her lips and his taste vanished, leaving her wondering if she'd imagined the entire thing. Emotions bounced through her like balls, soaring higher and higher until she felt weightless.

Oscar nestled against her, his head moving and his mouth rooting around, seeking her breast.

The primal need to put him to her breast pulled at her so strongly that she had to hold her arms rigid to prevent it happening.

Cal shifted against her. 'He looks like he's hungry.'

Panic hit her, sending burning acid surging into her gut. 'I don't have any formula in the house for you to give him.'

Confusion hovered on his face. 'Weren't you planning on breastfeeding?'

A gut-wrenching pain tore through her. Had he forgotten who she was? 'I…' She hauled in a breath, organising her thoughts. 'The plan was that Caroline and James would give Oscar his first feed.'

Stark understanding darted into his eyes and for a brief moment he closed them, shutting her out. She bit her lip at the short, sharp pain that momentarily dented her high.

When he opened his eyes again the wonder that had been so prominent when he'd handed Oscar to her had completely vanished. Instead, expediency had taken residence.

His jaw stiffened. 'But everything's changed now and all plans are void. I'll respect your wishes if you don't want to breastfeed him, but until we work out what's happening, I think it's best for you and for Oscar if you feed him.'

Hope soared through her that her role in Oscar's life might be secure. 'Best for me, too?'

His shoulders lifted and fell. 'Breastfeeding helps return the uterus to the pre-pregnant size and right now feeding him will help you deliver the placenta.'

His words slapped her with their pragmatism. The doctor from the war zone, where life diced with death every day, always took the practical approach. It had nothing to do with emotions at all.

A modern-day wet nurse. The thought chilled her as Curtis's snarl surfaced in her mind. 'You came in handy, Tess, you served a purpose.' Goose-bumps rose on her arms and her legs started to shake, the shudders rolling through her.

Could she feed this little man and then give him away? Oh, God, she wasn't sure she could. But she knew clear down to her solar plexus that she couldn't *not* breastfeed him.

Callum flicked open yet another towel and wrapped it around her shaking shoulders.

I'm not cold. Tess bit her lip and kept silent.

Callum knelt next to her. 'We need to get this placenta delivered and get you off this hard floor. Feeding Oscar will help the contractions start again. Do you need some help getting him to attach?'

Treat it like a job. She sucked in a fortifying breath. 'Do you know anything about breastfeeding?'

His mouth twitched up in a crooked grin. 'Only that his mouth needs to be open really wide.'

She laughed at his honesty and gazed down at Oscar, whose fists were starting to flail and whose mouth had opened wide, ready to attach. 'I think he's got that bit covered.' She lifted Oscar close, her knees supporting him against her breast, and he immediately turned and latched on with the suction of a limpet.

She gasped in shock and delight.

'What's wrong?' Callum's eyes darkened with unease.

She laughed. 'Nothing, it's just…'

'What?' His perplexed expression made him look so much like Oscar. 'If it hurts then he's not on properly.'

'It's not hurting, it's just not what I expected.' She stroked Oscar's cheek, watching how his little jaws worked, taking in colostrum and setting off a reaction inside her body to kick-start the making of milk. 'It's incredible how they know exactly what to do.'

'Genetic programming is a powerful thing.' Callum stood up and clapped his hands. 'Right. I'll get the sterilised scissors to cut the cord.'

Tess watched his retreating back, remembering how he'd clapped everyone into order prior to Theatre the night before. The man who had trailed the most delicious kiss across her lips had vanished without a trace. Instead, she had the doctor who viewed the situation as a 'job to be done', and she was merely the patient.

A tear slipped out of her eye, and she quickly brushed it away, surprised at its appearance. What was she thinking? No one met a man for the first time and then twenty-four hours later became a parent with him. Life didn't work like that.

Come on, Tess, you're a big girl. 'Happy families' has never been part of your life. You've accepted that.

But the baby in her arms, suckling at her breast, demanded she reconsider.

CHAPTER FIVE

CAL carried a cup of tea into Tess's room. Oscar, replete and asleep, lay in a basket close to Tess, who rested on the bed, leaning up against a large, square pillow. She wore a pink jersey top and her long legs stretched out of multicoloured pyjama shorts. Her short, tousled hair was still damp from the shower and her cheeks glowed with health and vitality. She looked sweet and tempting and good enough to eat.

You know she tastes sensational. The cup rattled in the saucer and he gripped it harder. Kissing Tess full on her soft lips had not been his most sensible decision. Then again, it hadn't actually been a decision. It had been more of an unconscious action—something that had just happened and had seemed the right thing to do at the time.

Wrong! The moment his lips had touched hers he'd wanted much more. He'd wanted to trace the way her top lip peaked in a bow and make her gasp. He'd wanted to snag her plump bottom lip with his teeth and draw it down so he could lose himself inside her warmth and savour what he knew would taste divine.

But she'd just given birth to his nephew and he'd been behaving like Neanderthal man. Hell, even Neanderthal man probably hadn't ravished a post-partum woman. *You always want things your own way, you only care about yourself.* Felicity's accusing voice echoed in his mind.

He hadn't thought of Felicity in a long time and he certainly didn't want to be thinking of her now. Flick belonged in the past. A past he wasn't proud of. But right now he needed to be thinking of the immediate future, of Oscar and Tess, and introducing his parents to their grandson.

Tess moved her gaze from Oscar and onto Callum's face, her eyes the colour and warmth of a latte. 'Oh, is that tea?'

'It is.' He set the cup and saucer down on her bedside table. 'Earl Grey with a dash of milk. I figured it's the least I could do after all that hard work.' The perfumed scent of bergamot spiralled up in a curl of steam.

'Thank you so much.' Her smile crinkled her eyes and a dimple appeared in her left cheek.

Again, a zing of appreciation flashed through him, completely out of proportion to the task. It was a cup of tea, not surgery under mortar attack.

She took a sip and breathed out a long sigh of contentment. 'There's nothing like a good cup of tea.'

'You're easily pleased.' He stood between Oscar's basket and the bed, his gaze moving between the baby and Tess. The moment his eyes settled on one of them he was torn by wanting to look at the other. He hated the sensation, and he pushed it away. He wasn't the Halroyd twin that gave in to examining feelings. Feelings only ripped you apart.

Tess put her half-empty cup down. 'You're frowning at me and looking a lot like Oscar. What's up?'

Her directness startled him and he fell back into old protective habits of being practical and 'doing' something. 'Drink your tea and then I'll take you and Oscar to hospital.'

She blinked as her mouth straightened and her lips pursed. 'Why do we need to go to hospital?'

He sighed and sat down on the bed. 'You've just had a baby. You need to be there for observation.'

She raised her light brown brows. 'We're the only doctors in town so Oscar and I are better off here with you to observe us. Besides, hospital is too noisy.'

Her fresh, tropical scent wrapped around him and the idea of looking after her and Oscar both appealed and appalled him. The doctor won over the man. 'What about general checks for you and Oscar?'

'Esther's the community midwife and she'll call by twice a day to do my checks, weigh Oscar and do his PKU test. So we're all sorted unless...'

What had he missed? 'Unless what?'

A wicked glint streaked across her eyes like a comet. 'Unless your skills are one hundred per cent doctoring and you can't cook because then we're in trouble. I'm absolutely starving.'

He bristled at her inference. 'I happen to be able to cook.'

She tilted her head. 'More than one meal?'

'Yes, more than one meal.' Indignation mixed with laughter.

She grinned. 'So we're sorted, then.'

Were they? She wasn't asking all that much, considering what she'd done for James and Carolyn. Oscar would soon be in Melbourne with his parents and Tess would be back on her feet and returning to her own life. Pushing down his concerns, he agreed.

'We're sorted except for telling our families. I'll go collect Mum and Dad and bring them back here so we can tell them together.' His rubbed his chin, his fingers rasping against stubble. 'What about your parents? You should ring them while I'm gone.'

Like a switch being flicked, her glow of euphoria dimmed as her hands fisted around the edge of the mattress. Her gaze, so often forthright and unerring, slid away and her head dropped.

Signs of hiding. 'They didn't know either, right?'

She slowly raised her head and looked at him, her eyes filled with sadness. 'Not exactly.'

Was she estranged from them? 'Well, either they know or they don't know—which one is it?'

She flinched and he immediately regretted his frank words. 'Tess, what's going on?'

Her top lip covered her bottom one and she dragged in a breath. 'I don't have any parents to tell.'

Her raw grief shadowed her eyes and he realised just how little he knew about her. 'I'm sorry. Losing your parents must have been really tough.'

She shook her head and blew her nose. 'I'm sorry, I'm usually fine talking about this…I guess it's just seeing Oscar and…' She hauled in a big breath and her hand reached out to stroke the baby's head. 'Oscar and I share a childhood in common—we're both orphans.'

Her words, so out of the blue, thundered through him, and settled uncomfortably in his chest. Words seemed inadequate so he drew a comparison instead. 'Carolyn's parents died when she was young, too.'

'That's how we met.' Tess's smile was filled with fondness and love. 'We were in the same group home and after a brief battle over a doll Carolyn and I became instant friends. We shared the doll and from then on we shared everything else. She was the most amazing person.' A far-away look settled in her eyes. 'Carolyn pushed me when I doubted myself, she laughed and cried with me and she was the sister I never had.'

The pieces of the puzzle started to fall into place. 'And you offered to give her the ultimate gift.'

She nodded and raised her gaze back to his. 'She and James wanted a child so badly and after six miscarriages and a diagnosis of a bicornuate uterus they had few options left to them. I was in a position to help. It all happened much more quickly than we'd imagined, only taking one cycle of IVF. I immediately took leave of absence from work and moved down here for the pregnancy so they could live it vicariously.'

Surprise rocked him, especially after her ultimatum to him yesterday. 'So you're not a local?'

Her chin rose. 'I like to think I am *now*. I've worked here for six months and James had tentatively offered me the position as second GP if I wanted to take it.'

If I wanted to take it. 'What position are you currently on leave from?'

She hesitated slightly before replying. 'I've deferred the offer of secondment to work at the UK Centre for Medical Research and Innovation in London.'

It was like being hit by an electric jolt and his gut flipped. If Tess had been offered this grant then she was extremely good at what she did. 'You're not serious? You're considering walking away from the cutting edge of medicine for a GP position in Narranbool?'

He couldn't keep the incredulous note from his voice. This was James all over again. Ignoring the big picture for the minutiae and wasting preciously needed skills in a backwater. Settling down was abhorrent to him. Life wasn't about wasting talent and he needed to show Tess that she belonged where she was needed. And that wasn't Narranbool.

Tess vibrated with anger and folded her arms across her chest, shooting Callum a look she hoped would burn him.

Did the man not see the baby that was under his nose? Could he only think about work? 'Everything is up in the air and nothing has been decided. Right now my most pressing concern isn't research. Right now we have to talk about Oscar.'

He stood up. 'Oscar will be just fine. My parents did a great job raising James and me.'

She thought of the grieving Halroyds who had looked so frail at the funeral and couldn't imagine that they were physically or emotionally up to raising a child—especially a baby whose first five years would be so demanding. Who would kick a footy to him? Who would chase him through the tunnel at the play park?

The fact Callum hadn't mentioned his role in Oscar's life rankled. 'I'm sure they did, but they're not thirty-five any more, unlike *you*.'

His shoulders stiffened. 'My job takes me to places no child should ever be.'

She threw up her hands. 'That's my point. Isn't it time to rethink your job so you can be part of Oscar's life?'

'I did that the *moment* you told me about Oscar.' Eyes the steel-grey colour of snow clouds flashed at her, their expression critical of her presumption. 'Usually between assignments with Frontline I stay overseas but now I'll return to Australia. I'll be very much a part of his life.'

She railed at the thought. 'In blocks of time. What about when you're away?'

A muscle spasmed in his cheek. 'Look, you don't have to worry, I'll sort it all out, but I promise you that Oscar will grow up secure.'

You don't have to worry. Her breath started to come in fast, small bursts. This childhood he'd just mapped out for Oscar was so far removed from the one the little boy would have had with Carolyn and James. 'How? How will you sort it out?'

He rubbed his temple as if it throbbed. 'I'll have to discuss it with Mum and Dad of course, but hiring a nanny seems an obvious choice to help support us.'

Her expression must have shown her horror because he immediately added, 'You can be involved in the choice of the nanny. In fact, we'd welcome your input.'

Don't do me any favours. She bit off the retort before it saw the light of day. She mustn't burn her bridges. This was her opportunity to be involved, to keep in contact with Oscar. She hooked her gaze with his. 'I could be his nanny.'

Derision slashed his face. 'Don't be ridiculous. You've put your life on hold for this family long enough. It's time you were back in the world that needs your medical skills, back in research.'

The code embedded in his statement was that anyone could raise a child. Not everyone could do medical research, and it was clear where he thought her duty lay.

And right then she realised that this man before her was so busy saving the world, so invested in the 'big picture' and driven by a sense of purpose that he had no clue that it was the everyday little things like love and laughter, healthy relationships, building sandcastles and separating household waste for recycling that actually saved the world one tiny step at a time.

How could she make him understand that his nephew needed him more than the world?

The front door slammed and Oscar flinched, his cry immediately loud and indignant.

'Cal? Are you there?' His father's voice, laced with confusion, called down the hall.

'Be there in a minute, Dad.' Callum walked toward the door.

Tess immediately picked up the howling Oscar, holding him upright, high on her shoulder and patting him gently. 'I'll come out and meet them.'

Callum shook his head at her offer. 'You just gave birth, Tess. You need to stay on the bed and I'll bring Mum and Dad to you.'

He walked toward the living room where he could hear his parents talking. 'Sorry, I was about to come and get you but I got held up.'

His mother leaned back against the soft leather of the couch, fanning herself. 'We'd spoken to everyone and it was time to leave.' Her normally tanned face looked pale. 'We thought we heard a baby.'

He dragged in a breath. This was it. He couldn't put it off any longer. 'You did, that's why I was held up. You remember the pregnant woman at the funeral?'

His father stood by the window, staring out into the dusty street. 'A friend of Carolyn's, wasn't she? I think I met her at their wedding.'

The wedding you missed. 'Yes, that's right. Well, she had a very quick labour and I delivered the baby in the bathroom an hour and a half ago.'

His mother's iris-blue eyes widened. 'Good heavens, an unexpected home birth.' She gave a tired smile. 'But a typical Cal moment. Excitement and drama follow you wherever you go.'

That's not the half of it.

'Or, if not, he goes out and finds it.' His father turned back from the window, an affectionate smile on his face. 'Although I don't understand why you brought her here rather than taking her directly to hospital.'

Two sets of inquisitive eyes stared straight at him. 'Tess's been living here with Carolyn and James. Come and meet her and baby Oscar.'

'Really? Your brother never mentioned that.' His mother struggled to rise to her feet. 'This couch is really far too soft.'

Patrick immediately crossed the room and extended his arm to his wife to use as a lever.

Cal frowned. For the first time his mother looked all of her sixty-five years. He wasn't used to thinking of her as old. She played tennis, enjoyed swimming and bushwalking and was an adventurous traveller. He shook off his concern—it had been a taxing day. He really hoped meeting Oscar would help her cope with the loss of James and Carolyn and caring for him would fill the hole in her life.

His parents followed him into Tess's room. Oscar was cradled in her arms fast asleep again, exhausted after his speedy entry into the world. The lump in his throat that had taken residence the moment he'd delivered Oscar thickened at the sight of Tess's head bent toward his nephew's, her blonde hair bright against the baby's dark strands.

Mother and child. The picture stamped against his heart.

Except they weren't. And they couldn't be.

Tess had signed on as a surrogate, not for life, and despite her well-intentioned but misguided offer to be Oscar's nanny, it was the Halroyds' turn to take over and nurture Oscar. Tess needed to go back to her pre-pregnant life. Back to her job.

A pang of regret flitted through him. He ignored it. His current life plan didn't have any room for family life. No, his focus was strictly on planning for Oscar, giving Tess some R and R, getting a new doctor installed in Narranbool, and getting the hell out of town.

Tess raised her head and smiled, but he caught the ripple of tension in her eyes.

He ushered his parents forward. 'Jennifer and Patrick Halroyd, meet Dr Tess Dalton.'

'I hear you've had a bit of excitement.' Patrick's hearty greeting sounded a bit forced.

His mother stumbled as she stepped toward the bed and Patrick wound his arm around her waist in a steadying and supportive gesture.

Tess's questioning gaze moved briefly to Callum's and then back to his parents. 'He arrived a bit earlier than expected.'

Jennifer glanced briefly at the baby, her smile fixed and polite but her attention slightly detached. 'He's lovely, dear.'

'Would you like to hold him?' Tess shifted her weight in preparation for passing Oscar over.

His mother was clearly taken aback by the question. 'That's all right, dear. I think he's best with you.'

Tess shot Cal a confused look.

'Mum, Dad, sit down, we need to talk.' Callum pulled some chairs around and sat on the bed next to Tess, facing his parents. 'Now, I know this is going to come as a shock, especially considering what's just happened, but there's no easy way to break it to you.'

'Spit it out, son.' Patrick's intelligent eyes fixed on Callum.

He took a deep breath, trying to work out the best way to tell the news. 'As you know, James and Carolyn had for a long time wanted—'

'Callum is trying to tell you that Oscar is James and Carolyn's baby. He's your grandson.' Tess extended her hand and touched Jennifer's arm.

'Wh-what?' Jennifer's mouth seemed to sag.

He should have felt cross that Tess had blurted it out but instead relief poured through him that the secret was finally out in the open. 'Tess has been a surrogate for them.'

Patrick slumped in his chair as Jennifer's hand gripped his forearm. 'We didn't know.' He turned to Callum, his tone accusatory. 'Did you know?'

He shook his head. 'No. Apparently the plan was to tell us when the child was born to keep the press at bay.' He sighed. 'You know James.'

Jennifer smiled weakly. 'You boys have always done things your own way, like your father.'

A hot pain burned under Callum's ribs. He remembered as kids how he and James had been inseparable, and how they'd finished each other's sentences when they'd been making big plans. But that had all finished three years ago.

Patrick leaned closer to the child. 'He looks just like Cal did. James was fair and Cal was dark, remember, Jen?'

Jennifer nodded, a memory glowing in her eyes. 'He's got Cal's serious frown, James's ears and Carolyn's nose.' She wriggled the fingers on her right hand as she stretched out to touch Oscar's head. 'I can't believe we have a grandson.'

Callum cleared his throat. 'So now we need to talk about getting Oscar to Melbourne and hiring a nanny and—'

Tess gave him a steely glare before leaning close to Jennifer. 'Would you like to hold him now?'

The new grandmother nodded and started shaking her right hand as if she was trying to increase her circulation. 'I can't take this in. I'd given up the idea of being a grandmother.' She spoke directly to Tess, her tone conspiratorial. 'Cal doesn't have a paternal bone in his body and I knew James and Carolyn had diffi-difficult…' She struggled over the word, which sounded almost muffled. 'Difficulites. But now to find out whis wittle baby iths…'

Callum's entire body went on alert at his mother's slurred words and he caught Tess's worried gaze. 'Mum, are you feeling OK?'

Patrick studied his wife. 'Darling, if I hadn't seen you with tea or water all day, I'd swear you'd been drinking.'

Jennifer's face took on a grey pallor and sweat trickled down her cheek. 'Feel thick.'

Tess immediately put the sleeping Oscar in his basket. 'Callum, get my bag.'

Somehow he managed to move his feet, the doctor in him having trouble surfacing and taking control—not quite able to override the worried son.

Tess had no such problems. 'Patrick, help me get Jennifer onto the bed.'

'What's going on?' Patrick moved to help his wife, fright in his dark grey eyes.

Callum unzipped the medical bag, reading the same diagnosis on Tess's worried face that he'd come to. 'Mum might be having a stroke.'

'No!' Patrick's fright snagged on the word and he gripped Jennifer's hand tightly.

'Sorry, Dad, move out of the way.' He needed access to his mother. 'Mum, can you squeeze my hands?'

His mother's small palms lay across the backs of his hands, their pressure soft. 'Press as hard as you can.'

A line of spittle dribbled out of her mouth as Jennifer concentrated. Callum looked up at Tess. 'Left is stronger than right.'

Tess nodded and ripped open an IV set, priming the tubing.

Don't stroke out on me, Mum, please. He forced his

voice to sound normal. 'I'm going to take your blood pressure and Tess is going to put an IV into your other arm.' With shaking hands he put the black Velcro cuff around her upper arm. 'Are you on any blood-pressure medication?'

She shook her head, her eyes dilated with fear.

The white ends of the stethoscope snapped into his ears and he concentrated on the whoosh and thump of arterial blood pounding against arteries. Damn it, it was way too high.

'Do I call an ambulance?' Patrick gripped his mobile phone.

Tess released the tourniquet, allowing the saline to flow into Jennifer's veins. 'The only two doctors in town are right here in this room, Patrick. Let us finish assessing her and then we can decide.'

'Right. Of course.' But the man who controlled a multimillion-dollar company didn't sound his usual certain self. Patrick started to pace.

Oscar started to cry.

'Drip's in and I recommend aspirin as an anticoagulant.' Tess turned, her gaze fixed on Oscar as if she wanted to pick him up.

Callum needed her. 'Dad, pick up the baby and stick your finger in his mouth.'

He caught the look on Tess's face as she swung back toward him, surprised that he actually knew something about babies. 'We need to reduce her BP, but slowly. I don't want to bring it down so fast that we under perfuse the brain.'

Tess chewed her bottom lip. 'What about oral nifedipine?'

'Good idea.' He turned back to his mother. 'Mum, I need to listen to the blood flow in your neck.' He placed the stethoscope on her carotid artery, listening for carotid brutis, the sound of a narrowed artery.

'I'm feeling a lot better now. It must have been the shock and the heat.' His mother put her hand up onto his arm. 'Please, don't fuss and turn it into a drama.'

He stilled. Her voice was its normal, crisp tone. 'I'm not fussing, Mum. Your blood pressure is sky high and you can't deny you were having trouble speaking. Squeeze my hands again.'

'Callum Patrick Halroyd, didn't you hear—?'

'Jenny, squeeze his hands.' Patrick's stern voice came from across the room.

'Oh, all right, but everyone is fussing.' Jennifer reluctantly squeezed Cal's hands with all her usual strength. 'How's that?'

'That's good, Mum. Normal pressure.' But the image of her dribbling, sagging mouth stayed with him.

Tess offered Jennifer a glass of water and watched her take the tablets. As she relieved her of the glass she sat down on the bed. 'Jennifer, I need you to undo your blouse so I can listen to your heart and chest.'

'You just had a baby, dear, you should be resting.'

Tess put her hand out toward Callum as if to say, Pass the stethoscope. But she kept her eyes firmly on Jennifer and a smile on her face. 'I can see where your son gets his determined streak from.'

'You can say that again.' Patrick rocked the now quiet Oscar in his arms.

Callum snorted at the same moment Jennifer did.

Tess's shoulders shook for a brief moment as if she

was stifling a laugh, but when she spoke her voice was sober. 'Jennifer, you've just had the classic symptoms of what is called a transient ischemic attack, or TIA. For five minutes blood had trouble getting to your brain and you had trouble speaking, your limbs were weak and I noticed when you walked into the room your balance was a bit wobbly. Fortunately, the blood supply is back to normal but this TIA is a big warning that you need to have treatment so that we can head off a full-blown stroke.'

Thank you, Tess. Callum watched the effect of Tess's carefully delivered words on his mother. Gone was the prickly woman. Instead, she leaned forward, her attention completely focused on Tess. 'Can you prevent me from having a stroke?'

'We will do our absolute best.' Tess squeezed her hand. 'Callum will organise for you to get to Melbourne for a couple of days in hospital and a battery of tests.'

Jennifer looked over her shoulder at Patrick and Oscar. 'Can't you do them here?'

Cal ran his hand through his hair. 'No, Mum, Narranbool's too small and you'll mostly likely need to see a vascular surgeon and have an operation to clear out the blockage in the artery in your neck.'

Tess sighed. 'Callum's quite correct. Although we could do the ECG, the blood tests and an X-ray, we don't have a CT scanner or a surgeon.'

'Dad, order the helicopter.' Callum started making lists in his head.

'Will do.' His father passed the baby over to Callum so he could use his phone.

Oscar's eyelids stayed closed but the flickers of REM

sleep made them twitch. Even though he was yet to have his first bath he smelt baby-fresh. Cal's arms instinctively tightened around him.

Patrick reached for his phone and then stopped, suddenly struck by something. 'You're coming with us, Cal?'

He shook his head. 'Sorry, Dad, until I can get another doctor up here, I'm staying. Tess needs some time off to recuperate but we'll send a nurse with you to monitor Mum.'

'Right. You're staying here. Good.' Patrick clapped his hands and immediately turned to Tess. 'With Jenny needing tests and probable surgery, the best place for Oscar right now is here with you. I know you've already done an incredible thing for this family but can I ask you this huge favour and leave Cal as collateral to help you out?'

No, Dad, no! Cal opened his mouth to object.

'Of course I'll help.' Tess's soft voice readily agreed.

How could everything have gone this pear-shaped? Oscar should have been born in Melbourne, his mother should be her normal, vital self and able to care for a baby, and he should have been spending the coming day or two in this house alone. Instead, he was going to be sharing it with a woman who with one flash of her determined chocolate eyes both heated his blood and infuriated him all at the same time.

How the hell was he going to deal with that?

CHAPTER SIX

TESS listened to the burring and clicking of the frogs. The sounds floated on the night air from the billabong that ran behind the back of the block, a lazy diversion of the Lachlan River. A slight breeze fluttered though the open sash of the window, moving the thick, hot air, attempting to take the edge off the stifling heat. Even so, hardly anyone in Narranbool would be sleeping tonight. She knew *she* was having trouble getting to sleep.

She sighed, knowing the heat had nothing to do with her insomnia. Neither did Oscar, who lay in the basket beside her fast asleep, dressed only in a cloth nappy and a cotton singlet, the nightlight casting a soft, warm glow over him.

Her insomnia had everything to do with Callum.

Her ears strained past the frogs and the crickets, past the moths batting at the veranda light, and out into the night, listening for his return. She was pathetic. He was a grown man, a doctor out on call, not a teenager late home.

But she missed his presence in the house—the way

he opened every kitchen cupboard door when he cooked, the creaking sound of the hall floorboards under his feet as he settled a fractious Oscar, and his infrequent but special full-bodied laugh that stole his serious demeanour and gave her a glimpse of a side of him that usually lay hidden.

It was crazy to miss a man who'd had been at work more than he'd been at home, but that didn't stop her lying awake, listening and waiting.

The door clicked open and then closed gently, the sound muffled. A slight thump followed and then the familiar creak of floorboards radiated down the hall. Butterflies of excitement fluttered in her stomach.

Callum paused at her open door, his shoes dangling from the fingers of his right hand. Dark stubble covered his cheeks, his hair fell forward and his shirtsleeves were rolled up to his elbows. He looked tired, dishevelled and totally gorgeous.

'Still awake? Oscar been fussy?' His baritone voice sounded weary.

She smiled. 'He woke at eleven, fed and went back to sleep. I guess the evaporative cooler helps.'

Callum pushed off the door post and walked into the room, his exhaustion almost rising off him in waves. 'It's certainly cooler in here than the rest of the house.' Resting a hand on the edge of the basket, he stared at the sleeping baby. 'I swear he's longer than he was five hours ago.'

Tess laughed. 'I used to think it was nonsense when parents said babies grew in their sleep but now I agree with them. I can't get over how much he's changed in a week.' A twinge of regret lanced her. In a short seven days Oscar had already changed and he would keep changing, but how many growth spurts would she be around to see?

'Any luck with tracking down a locum?' Callum deftly changed the subject.

He'd asked the same question daily and she'd been on the phone most of the evening. 'I've got the promise of a possibility in three weeks.'

'Three weeks?' The words came out as a combination of incredulity and resignation.

She splayed her hands out in front of her. 'The good news is that next week I can go back to work.'

He spun around from Oscar's basket so fast she thought he'd fall over. 'No. You need a few weeks off before you throw yourself back into work.'

She read the care on his face and cosy warmth spread through her.

He rubbed his temple. 'Plus with Mum only just out of hospital after her carotid endarterectomy, it's going to be a few weeks before she's up to managing Oscar.'

His words acted like a spray of icy cold water and she shivered, unable to stop the reaction. Curtis's unwanted voice boomed again in her head. *You filled a need, Tess.*

Pushing away the toxic words, she heard Callum continuing to speak.

'The practice is officially going up for sale because Narranbool needs a permanent doctor, not just a locum.'

Pain pierced her heart. She'd expected the sale as part of the estate but not the speed with which it was taking place. She wanted to yell out, I might want to be that doctor, but right now she didn't know. Narranbool was closer to Oscar than London but Melbourne held the biggest pull.

With great effort she swallowed the unspoken words because she had a pretty good idea what his reaction to that statement would be. Right now it was too hot and too late to argue so she put it off for another time.

Instead, she offered him the chance to debrief, knowing he didn't enjoy the role of being Narranbool's GP. 'So you've had a busy night? Sit down and tell me all about it because with this heatwave I feel a bit cut off from the real world. I can't wait for it to finish so Oscar and I can go out for a walk.'

He grimaced. 'It's shocking weather for babies and the elderly.' He swung his legs up onto the bed, which creaked under his weight, and he leaned back on a bank of pillows so he could catch the cooler air from the fan. 'I've had to admit Mrs Rubenstein. Her lungs are full of fluid and this heat isn't helping her cardiac failure.'

Tess sighed. 'Poor Ruth. She's probably drunk too much just trying to keep cool, and between her eighty-five-year-old heart and kidneys it was all too much.'

He nodded. 'That's about the strength of it. Ken's got her on a strict fluid balance chart and by tomorrow the Lasix should have done the trick and she'll be breathing more easily. I'll check her in the morning.' He turned and faced her. 'Shouldn't you be asleep?'

Again his consideration cloaked her with its tantalising warmth.

He sighed. 'Oscar will be awake again in a few short hours.'

It's consideration for Oscar, you fool. She forced her lips into a smile. 'You're sounding like an expert parent.'

He ran his hand through his hair. 'I'm so far removed from that it's not funny. Most blokes have a minimum of nine months to get used to the idea. I got less than twenty-four hours.'

She wasn't sure whether she heard regret in his voice or not, so she asked the question that had been demanding an answer ever since she'd met him. 'Did you see children in your future?'

He shook his head. 'Not really.'

His answer only surprised her because of the qualifier. 'That means you must have thought about it at some point.'

He rubbed his left palm with his thumb, a gesture she'd noticed he made whenever he was formulating an answer. 'It's my experience it generally comes up for discussion in a relationship.'

'Ah.'

His eyes simmered with indignation. 'What's that supposed to mean?'

'It means the woman brings up the future and children in discussion, and discovers that her partner doesn't actually feel the same.'

He shifted as if he was uncomfortable. 'And you know this for a fact?

She shrugged. 'It's the twenty-first century. Every woman in her late twenties to thirties knows it.'

Dark grey eyes scanned her face with the probing skills of an ultrasound. 'That sounds personal.'

Tess, our relationship was convenient to both of us. It was never going to go the full catastrophe of marriage and children. She brushed her fringe out of her eyes, brushing away Curtis's voice. She didn't want to talk about Curtis. 'It's more of a comment on society in general.'

'Really?' He didn't sound like he believed her. 'Well, Felicity viewed it as me being my usual selfish self.' His voice had an unusual edge.

She studied his suddenly tense jaw. Over the last week he'd been working flat out at the practice, as well as helping her, even insisting on getting up and changing Oscar's nappy at two a.m. before she fed him. 'I'd call you headstrong, determined and an adrenaline junky but…' she grinned, softening her words '…selfish wouldn't be a description I'd use.'

'Gee, thanks.'

His wry smile trailed along his strong cheekbones, making her gut freefall. 'My pleasure.' She rolled onto her side to face him directly. 'So exactly why were you accused of being selfish?'

He sighed. 'You're not going to let this go, are you?'

Not on your life. She forced her voice to sound light. 'I figure that as you've seen me at my most exposed when you delivered Oscar, the least you can do is tell me a bit about yourself.'

'Put like that, I guess you have a point. But this story isn't pretty and it does nothing for me as a character reference.'

His sombre voice vibrated with a regret that struck her as completely out of character for his usual 'action man' persona. Intrigue simmered inside her but if she was truthful with herself she would have accepted any information about him, even if it was just a favourite colour. She was desperate to know what made him tick. 'Well, now you *have* to tell me.'

He rolled away from her, lying on his back, his eyes fixed on the slowly turning ceiling fan, deliberately avoiding her gaze.

The sudden movement spoke volumes and she had to stop herself from reaching out and touching his arm in a gesture of comfort.

'Felicity and I did everything back to front and everything way too fast. We met and by the end of the first month more than just her toothbrush was in my bathroom vanity. Piece by piece, she'd completely moved in within sixty days. Without consultation she sublet her own place to save money as she was preparing to open a business.' He sighed. 'Hindsight is a wonderful thing and I should have dealt with it right there and then, but as surgical registrar at the beck and call of two consultants I had no time to call my own. I'd arrive home and crash. Flick would be there with a hot meal, a glass of wine, and home became a place I could just collapse and recuperate.'

He glanced at her, as if assessing her reaction and expecting an 'all men are bastards' look, but Tess kept her expression neutral. She already had Felicity pegged.

He brought his hands up behind his head. 'She arranged and threw dinner parties, she organised my parents' annual charity ball, she redecorated the apartment and alphabetised my filing cabinet.'

Tess couldn't help herself. 'She sounds like a fabulous PA.'

He flashed her an unreadable look. 'Except she wasn't a PA. She was my girlfriend.'

Tess raised her brows. 'A girlfriend who willingly created an oasis for you. And then I'm guessing she hit you with the bill.'

'A bill I didn't pay.' He ran his hand through his hair. 'She wanted marriage, a family and me in a Collins Street practice. I'd just been offered the Frontline job, one that we—one that I'd worked incredibly hard to get, so I suggested we wait.'

Tess knew the answer before she asked the question. 'And she wasn't keen on that idea?'

His short, derisive laugh sounded harsh against the cricket's song. 'That's the understatement of the year. And by this stage she'd roped in allies, my parents and Jam— My friends thought I was mad and passing up the best catch a man and doctor could have.'

The half-spoken name of his twin had been almost imperceptible, but Tess caught it. Callum rarely mentioned James and she'd gleaned that since he'd been working in Africa contact had been minimal. Carolyn and James hadn't ever said much about Callum and she'd never really given it much thought because she'd not met him. But now, having met his parents, it seemed strange that the twins had not been closer.

What had James thought of Callum's plans? What had he thought of Felicity? 'But Felicity wasn't really a partner, was she?'

His head moved slowly against the pillow, his shoulders and the rest of his body following until he faced her. When he opened his mouth the words came out stony. 'In the eyes of the world she was my de facto.'

She tugged at her ear. 'Granted, you let a situation slide, but did you at any time promise her what she wanted?'

'Lack of action on my part made it implicit.' Guilt hovered around him.

Tess suddenly needed him to see Felicity for who she really was—a woman who'd seen him and decided she wanted him as her husband, no matter what. 'Did you ever ask her to do any of the things she did?'

His pupils expanded into inky discs. 'Hell, no. I *liked* my apartment the way it was. I encouraged her to work as an interior designer, to start her own business, to be her own person, and I sure as hell never asked her to collect my dry-cleaning.'

He puffed out a long breath. 'Anyway, it's long over and I'm never putting myself up for that sort of acrimony again. I'm not moving in with anyone until we've had a very long dating period and the expectations on both sides are well understood.'

He rolled off his side and onto his back, closing his eyes and closing the conversation. 'I went to Africa and I heard she married within the year.'

Of course she did. Tess had met women like Felicity. As long as the man fitted the correct socio-economic demographic, they were fairly interchangeable.

She looked down at him, wanting to tell him it was time to let go of the guilt, but his long, thick lashes, which brushed his tanned cheeks, sidetracked her, as did the deep crevices carved around his eyes. She watched his chest rise and fall, his pectoral muscles straining against his shirt, hinting at the strength that lay beneath the fine cotton.

Squeezing her hand shut, she held it fisted to prevent it from reaching out. But her fingers tingled, longing to open the small pearl buttons, sneak under the soft fabric and feel the beat of his heart against her palm.

The man was exhausted but all she could think about

was what it would be like to touch him. Taste him. Feel his body curled around hers. She swallowed and took in a deep breath. This was insanity. Callum wasn't interested in a relationship. He was considerate and caring but she was nothing more to him than the woman who cared for his nephew until he could get his real plan into action. The plan that involved Oscar in Melbourne, being cared for by his parents, a nanny and occasionally himself between 'world-saving missions'.

His breathing deepened and slowed as sleep quickly claimed him—the skill all medical personnel quickly developed, that of maximising all opportunities for precious sleep. She took the gift of being able to gaze at him openly and committed to memory the small scar under his chin, the curve of his solid calves, the way his long surgeon's fingers tapered to well-kept nails. She breathed in his masculine scent of sandalwood and sweat, and recalled in her mind the touch of his lips against hers. Uncertainty tainted her life but right now this man was real and she drank the sight of him in.

Slowly, the edges of her vision became fuzzy and her eyes fluttered closed and her dreams took over, filling her with the man who fascinated her so much.

A knocking noise tried to break into Tess's dream but she resisted surfacing from the full-colour movie where she was the leading lady and Callum was the leading man. Along with the dream she'd had the most amazing sleep she'd had since...since she could remember.

The blinds at the window banged wildly against the frame as a strong, chilly wind blew into the room. The cool change had arrived. Blissfully fresh, brisk air swooped over her and she snuggled into the bed with a contented sigh, savouring the joy of being cocooned under a sheet, a feeling unknown for the last few nights.

Delicious warmth radiated from her thighs, out across her bottom, tracking along her back, tracing over her belly and spreading out like a fan over her chest, before finishing with a focus point of splayed heat directly over her right breast. A moan of pleasure rolled out of her as she stretched out, her left leg brushing against something that rested between her legs, pinning her right leg to the mattress.

A long, hard, weight.

Sleep vanished. She forgot to breathe.

Callum's left leg lay between her legs, his knee firmly pressing against her thigh and his hand curved gently around her breast. He moved against her, deep in sleep, his head burrowing into her neck, and his breath caressing her skin.

His sigh of contentment washed over her as his arms tightened around her, closing the small gap between them. His hips cupped her behind which curved into his lap, his arousal hard against her despite two layers of clothing between them. Her breasts tingled under his hand, her blood pumping the stirrings of pleasurable need down to the smallest cells deep inside her.

He's asleep, you should move.

But she didn't want to. She didn't want to give up this glorious sensation of being wrapped up in his body like a precious gift. She didn't want to give up the feeling of being cherished. It had been a long time since she'd been held and even *that* had turned out to be an illusion.

He smelt divine—a chaotic aroma of musk and sweat, and citrus and mint. She'd dreamed of this and reality intensified every moment.

The window blind rakishly hit the frame with a metallic clatter. Oscar's incensed cry rent the air.

Callum twitched and groaned and then stilled. She felt tension enter his body and travel along every muscle, until he was taut against her as he realised his position.

'Hell.' His voice, rough with sleep, grazed her soul like gravel. 'Sorry.'

He rolled away so fast it was as if she was contaminated. Cold air immediately slugged her, its touch no longer refreshing but jagged with ice. Every part of her screamed with loss.

'I'll change him.' Callum's feet hit the floor and he swept the howling and hungry infant into his arms.

He quickly marched out of the room, taking all Tess's silly make-believe fantasy with him. She pulled the sheet over her head as embarrassment swept through her.

She lived in the real world, a place where fantasies didn't belong. She knew this as intimately as she knew that life required oxygen. As a child she'd dreamed of belonging to a family but that had never happened. As an adult in her early twenties she'd dreamed of creating a family. But Curtis had buried those hopes as effectively as concrete buried soil.

Tonight she'd let a dream convince her she still had a chance at the family she wanted, but she had stars in her eyes if she thought Callum was going to want to join her in her castle in the sky. He was too busy saving the world to contemplate a relationship, and he didn't see her as anything more than his nephew's temporary caregiver.

He was the man she knew she could never have.

CHAPTER SEVEN

THE sharp point of the nappy pin pierced Cal's thumb and he swallowed another curse to add to the many he'd silently uttered in the last five minutes. He couldn't believe that he'd just woken up wrapped around all the softness that was Tess. The fact he'd managed to walk from the room was a miracle.

He hadn't spooned with a woman in years. Sure, he'd had sex but that was all it had been. Sex and no strings. Since Felicity he'd avoided long-term relationships, avoided entrapment, which had been easy given his lifestyle. Most Frontline staff had similar views and their work didn't allow for commitment to anything other than the job. And the job demanded one hundred per cent and then some.

But tonight not only had he spooned and slept like a log, he'd actually talked about Flick, something he never did. Tess had managed to sneak under his guard and that unnerved him. The woman was way too insightful as well as being as sexy as hell. He'd almost told her about James but fortunately had stopped himself. That was one secret he planned to keep.

Oscar's watery eyes sparkled up at him as he hic-coughed before enthusiastically sucking his fist.

'Nearly finished, mate. Food's coming.'

He heard the post-office clock chime five. A new day was dawning, his ninth day in Narranbool. *Nine days with Tess*. He might hate Narranbool but spending time with Tess was no hardship. He'd never met anyone quite like her. She was a mixture of practicality and gene-rosity, and she could get him to laugh—something he'd forgotten how to do.

Lighten up, Cal. James had always been the one to make him laugh. But James had gone and now their three years of estrangement circled his heart like barbed wire.

He closed the Velcro tabs on the nappy cover and manoeuvred the baby's kicking legs into the growsuit. Clicking the snaps closed, he then picked up Oscar and laid him over his shoulder. The warmth and weight of the baby soaked into him and his heart expanded more.

Tess had said a doctor could be here in three weeks. He desperately hoped that was so. Tess needed a holiday before flying to London and he wanted a couple of weeks with Oscar, his parents and the nanny, settling them in before taking up the two-month rotation with Frontline he'd promised to lead.

He will grow so much while you're away.

He steeled himself against the voice. As a surgeon he had a gift he had to share, and sometimes sacrifices had to be made for the greater good.

Tess's heart rate picked up as she walked out the back door and admired the view. Callum's taut backside stuck out of the car, his shorts pulled tightly across firm, muscular buttocks. He'd left the house half an hour ago to do a job. She heard a thump and a muttered oath.

She tried to peer around him into the car but his broad shoulders blocked the view and she couldn't see what he was doing. 'My hands are smaller, if that will help.'

Callum backed out of the car, his face a mixture of frustration and incredulity, his hand shaking a thick book of instructions at her. 'My surgeon's hands can do all sorts of tricky things in small places, thank you very much. But this car seat is harder to connect than plugging Vince's bleeding ulcer!'

Tess smothered a laugh. Her in-control hotshot surgeon was out of his depth, derailed by a baby car seat. She couldn't resist teasing him. 'I know that blokes don't like to ask for instructions so I'm offering so that you can save face.'

He shot her a superior look. 'Too late. I've done it now, but by all means check my work.'

She smiled. 'Well done, but I think Craig at the garage is the best person to check it. He's a qualified fitter.'

Callum raked his hand through his hair, clumping the strands into spikes of black and silver. 'You're telling me I just spent thirty frustrating minutes working out tether straps, anchor straps and gated buckles, and this town has someone who can do it?'

She nodded, this time letting herself smile broadly. 'Sure we do. Narranbool isn't quite the backwater you seem to imagine it is.' His attitude toward the town puzzled her and it got under her skin. She loved it here. James and Carolyn had loved it and she found it hard to understand his attitude. He didn't need to love Narranbool but why did he need to hate it so much?

His snort evaporated into the clear blue sky of the early autumn morning as his hands gripped his hips in an aggressive stance. 'And you didn't mention Craig to me because…?'

It struck her that they were having their first domestic argument. 'Because, action man, you scooped up the car seat and strode outside full of intent. Tell me…' She fixed him with a straight gaze. 'If I'd tried to stop you, would you have listened?'

Callum opened his mouth and then closed it, his grey eyes filling with a hint of discomfiture and the suggestion of a smile twitching his lips. 'I'll concede I probably would have said, "It's a car seat, how hard can it be?"'

She raised her hand and he slapped her palm in a high five as his baritone laughter swirled around her, taunting her with how it would feel to hear that laugh every morning. She promptly closed her mind to pointless thoughts and focused instead on the day ahead.

'If you whiz down to the garage for a quick check, I'll get Oscar ready for our first outing.' Excitement rushed through her at the chance to leave the house and garden that had been her sanctuary now for over a week.

He raised his jet-black brows as a supercilious look crossed his face. 'I'm assuming I don't have to book and there won't be a queue?'

There it was again—a jibe at the town. 'Craig's pretty busy at this time of year, servicing the farmers' headers, but play nice and he'll happily help you.'

He didn't react to her admonishment, instead he fished his keys out of his pocket. 'So where did you have in mind for this inaugural outing? The park is burned to a crisp, the waterhole is lacking water and the art gallery-cum-museum is closed on Tuesdays.'

His resentment of Narranbool fizzed between them; his reaction to the town almost pathological and she had no idea why. *For as long as I can remember I've looked beyond this 'wide brown land'.* How could twins be so very different? James had loved the district and the people.

But different they were. Where James had been happy to sit and chew the fat, Callum needed to be constantly busy. He had no idea how to kick back and smell the roses, or, in Narranbool's case, the aroma of the wattle.

She watched him jiggle the keys while he waited for her answer and an idea embedded itself in her mind. She had just the place where he could be very busy and at the same time see a new side to the area. A place where she could keep a promise. 'It's a surprise. But fill the truck with diesel and I'll pack some food and water. We're going out for the day.'

The four-wheel-drive's tyres crunched over the compressed red-rock road, and Tess gripped the hold bar as Callum changed down into low gear to ford yet another dry creek bed. Gnarly river gums clung to the low banks, their roots rambling far from their bases to catch what little water came their way. Mistletoe dangled from tall branches like chandeliers hanging from a ceiling and the distinctive leaves of the eucalypt seemed greener against the white bark that hid a deep red wood.

'This reminds me of the Flinders Ranges. Dad used to take James and me out camping and the first job was to find a decent fallen limb of red gum for the campfire.'

Tess turned toward him and smiled. 'It sounds wonderful. Like a *Boy's Own* adventure.'

He gripped the wheel as he manoeuvred the truck back onto the road. 'I didn't mind it, although the night the creek flooded was a bit hairy.'

She checked Oscar, who was safely strapped into his car seat, unperturbed by the bouncing vehicle. 'Somehow I can't quite picture Halroyds camping.'

He grinned. 'Despite Dad being able to afford to travel in five-star comfort from about the time I was eight, he insisted we do the same things he'd done with his father. Pop was a bushie so I can cast a mean line, fillet a fish, pitch a tent and find approximate south without a compass.'

She couldn't keep the wistful tone out of her voice. 'Traditions are important, especially today with life changing so fast.'

'Hmm, I guess they are.'

He didn't sound like he'd given it much thought and that didn't surprise her. He was too busy with the big world picture to think about the small things that underpinned it.

Callum pressed the button for the windscreen cleaner to make a dent in the red dust. 'So what sort of family traditions do you have?' The moment the question left his mouth a horrified look scored his face. 'I'm sorry, I didn't think.'

She shrugged her shoulders, wanting him to feel better. 'That's OK. I've invented a few of my own and one foster-family I lived with always went to the beach at dawn on Easter Sunday to watch the sunrise.'

He raised his forefinger off the steering-wheel to indicate the vivid red and brown of the outback that surrounded them. 'That one's a bit hard in Narranbool when you're a thousand kilometres from the beach.'

She thought of the pink rays of first light creeping across the water, giving Narranbool an unusual softness before the harsh light exposed its dust and rugged edges. She hugged herself. 'Dawn over the river is pretty special. You should try it before you leave town.'

He abruptly shook his head. 'It's not something I'd set the alarm for, but going on Oscar's last couple of mornings I'll be up anyway.'

She tried to smile but she hated the fact that Oscar wouldn't grow up knowing where he'd been born. 'There you go, then. It can be your first tradition with your nephew.' The words came out with a disapproving edge.

He glanced at her, his eyes keen and all-seeing. 'I promise you I will take Oscar camping when he's older.'

And where will I be then? 'Make sure you do that.' She turned to check Oscar again but his eyes were closed, the rocking of the vehicle soothing him to sleep.

'So what traditions did you invent?'

His unexpected question startled her. Why had she mentioned she'd invented traditions? She hadn't thought when she'd spoken, she'd only wanted to make him feel better when he'd thought he'd upset her.

She didn't want to talk about traditions. Talking about them meant talking about Curtis. Her silly attempts at family traditions had been as ridiculous as her belief that she and Curtis had had a future together.

But Callum's gaze had a determined streak of silver to it and she was locked in a car with him for at least another ten minutes before they arrived at the settlement. 'Nothing as fabulous as campfires in creek beds.' She pushed the half-loaded CD into the player, ending the conversation.

Surprised at Tess's blatant attempt to halt the conversation, Cal bided his time, watching the sunlight pick up the blonde highlights in her short hair, the long-layered cut giving her a tomboyish look. She'd lost her round face of pregnancy and her thinner face made her high cheekbones more pronounced. She glowed with wellbeing and an energy that made him want to reach out and capture it, and hold it close.

Why hasn't someone else caught her? That question had kept circling in his head since she'd told him about her decision to be a surrogate. But between taking care of Oscar and taking care of the town, the chance to ask her hadn't presented itself.

A few moments ago she'd been so gung-ho about the need for traditions and now she'd clammed up. He pressed the 'stop' button on the CD player, cutting the music. 'You just finished telling me how traditions are important and now you've gone silent on yours.'

Her jaw tensed. 'Like I said, they were nothing so grand as your outback adventures.'

An unexpected flash of hurt burned in her eyes for a moment. He recognised it for what it was. A pain instilled in her soul by someone she'd cared for. 'Someone make fun of your traditions, Tess?'

She stared straight ahead for a moment, her shoulders so stiff they could have been starched. 'You're a man. You're not supposed to be perceptive.'

He wasn't falling for that old chestnut—the provocative statement that started an argument and avoided the original topic. 'Ah, but I love to break the stereotype.' He gave her a smile. 'Come on, spit it out. It can't be more of a disaster than Flick and me.'

'Yeah, it can be.' She slowly turned to face him. 'You know how Felicity moved herself into your life? Well, Curtis moved me into his.'

The strong need to know all about this guy surprised Cal. He didn't usually take much interest in other people's lives. *You did with James.* He closed his ears to the voice and focused on Tess. 'How did he move you into his life?'

'I fell for the cliché.' Her breath shuddered out on a ragged sigh. 'He told me we belonged together.'

He could see her beating herself up and he hated that. 'That would have been a pretty powerful thing to be told when you'd grown up without a family to belong to.'

Appreciation filled her large, brown eyes. 'It was an aphrodisiac. I was at Sydney Uni in fourth year. It was my birthday and I was missing Carolyn and my foster-family dreadfully. Curtis and I met in the library. He was the same age but a year behind me, having repeated first year as many students did.'

She compressed her lips. 'He was a natural charmer, he had a fabulous bedside manner, but he struggled with the course work. I gave him some help with pharmacology and he got the highest mark he'd ever got.'

'And you started dating?' The rhetorical question rolled easily off his tongue.

She nodded. 'We did. We dated and we studied

together. I'd never had a study partner—Carolyn was involved in art and drama at high school and I'd always hit the books alone. All of a sudden I had someone to share the grind with as well as the joy of learning, but it was much more. I came out of my cave of study and a met a side of the world I hadn't really experienced.'

She laced her hands together. 'Curtis was well liked by everyone and effusive with his praise for me. With his arm firmly around my waist, he'd introduce me to his friends, telling them how important I was to him.' Tossing her head slightly, she swallowed hard. 'It turns out my interpretation of important was very different from his.'

He heard her pain and an unexpected knife of fury sliced through him, directed at this man who had hurt her so badly. 'What happened?'

She rubbed her palms against her shorts. 'After a year we moved as a couple into a shared house situation. I was on a scholarship and had a part-time job but Curtis struggled to work and keep up his course work. He cut back his work hours and it seemed logical at the time to combine our incomes and live off that.'

Callum bit off the retort that his mouth wanted to blurt out. This guy sounded like a user.

Tess trailed her finger along the dashboard. 'As soon as I graduated Curtis suggested we move into our own place, just the two of us. I'd always lived in someone else's home and I'd never had my very own space so the idea really appealed to me.' A wry smile hovered around her lips. 'I loved that apartment and the area. I guess the analysts would call it nesting but whatever the name, I set about creating something special for the two of us, an oasis from the world, and I started my first family traditions.' She picked up her water bottle and took a long drink.

He recognised the stalling technique—he'd used it often enough himself. 'And at that point, life was good?'

Her brown eyes, so large in her elfin face, blinked. 'I was deluded enough to think it was. In Curtis's final year he asked me to completely support him financially so he could get the best opportunity to pass well and join me in the intern programme at Royal Sydney.'

He heard his sharp intake of breath and instantly regretted it.

Her eyes flashed with a combination of self-righteousness and embarrassment. 'Before you say how dumb I was, he rightfully pointed out that we'd been together for four years, we were solid as a couple and the rewards of hard work were about to pay off. I saw a golden pathway for us both, stretching toward the future.

'But, like they say, everything that glitters isn't gold, and it turns out my pathway was sprayed with soluble paint.' Her laughter, usually so joyous and chiming, was short, sharp and derisive. 'Apparently I was *very* important to him that year. I helped him pass, I financially supported his affair with Kim, the aspiring model, and the moment he qualified he moved with her to Perth.'

His gut feeling about this guy had been right. He thumped the steering-wheel hard, wishing it was the lying, cheating scum of the man who had hurt her so badly. 'The guy is a snake.'

She nodded slowly. 'Yeah. He shed his skin and left. But the thing that hurts the most is that I had no idea. No idea that I was just a useful piece in that phase of his life and that I could be discarded the moment I was no longer required.'

Her anguish swirled around him. He wanted to hug her, make her feel better, but all he could do on this narrowing track was give her words. 'Love blinds us.'

She breathed out a short puff through her nose. 'Yeah, well, Curtis gave me 20-20 vision.' She straightened in her seat. 'So that's my sordid little tale and since then I've thrown myself into work with no strings or attachments. Some of us aren't cut out to have families and knowing that meant I was in the ideal position to help Carolyn and James.'

He ignored the aching ripple that moved through him at her belief she wouldn't have a family of her own. Talent and skill came at a cost. 'Except for the small matter of deferring a major research job.'

She turned again to check Oscar. 'Sometimes the job has to take a back seat for the people you love.'

He frowned. 'But when the job helps so many more, then surely it takes precedence? Your research saves lives.'

She gave him a long look with a hint of pity in her eyes.

He slowed and pulled on the handbrake, glad they'd just reached a fence with a closed gate and he had an excuse to get out of the truck. He hated being the recipient of that look. It was reminiscent of the one James had levelled at him the last time they'd spoken.

'Nothing is ever that black and white, Callum.'

His chest tightened. 'Yes, it is. It has to be.' He ground the words out against a hammering ache in his head. It had to be or he'd lost a brother for nothing.

CHAPTER EIGHT

CAL read the sign on the gate as he opened it and then walked back to the vehicle, swinging up into the driver's seat. 'I'm assuming as you've directed me to here that you have a permit and we have permission to enter Aboriginal land?'

Tess nodded as she slipped a dummy into a crying Oscar's mouth in an attempt to keep him happy for a few more minutes. 'We're welcome, so no dramas.'

He shoved the gearstick into first and moved forward just beyond the gate before jumping out again to close it behind him. He mightn't live in Australia but he knew the outback rules and *not* shutting the gate was a cardinal sin.

By the time he'd hooked the chain over the post, Oscar was screaming his lungs out.

His gut tightened. He hated it when the baby cried—the sound made him feel helpless and he never felt helpless. He was the one in control. Always in control. He jumped back into the truck. 'Do you want to feed him now?'

'We're less than five minutes away.' She tried again

with the dummy. 'It would be easier to feed him at the settlement.'

He gunned the engine and sped down the more even track, his eyes glued to the road, determined not to look at Tess's T-shirt. Oscar's crying had affected her too and she'd involuntarily let down milk. Now her shirt clung to her round and heavy breasts.

'And people think babies need changing a lot.' She gave an embarrassed laugh. 'I can't turn up looking like this.' She fumbled in the bag at her feet and quickly drew the wet shirt over her head and replaced it with a dry one before setting about the complicated procedure of changing her bra under the shirt.

His knuckles shone white and the steering-wheel threatened to snap in half in his hands he was gripping it so tight. She seemed to have no idea the effect her body had on him and it had to stay that way. Just as life had thrown them together for a short time, it was about to throw them apart again as they headed off to their respective lives.

A group of children came running toward the truck as a cluster of rundown concrete houses came into view. Tess wound down her window and gave a big wave. 'We're here.'

He stared at the lack of glass in some of the houses' windows and at empty doorframes, shocked by the conditions. 'How many people live here?'

'About eighty on and off, depending on the time of the year. There are four settlements similar to this spread out over the area.' She unclipped the straps on the car seat and lifted the fractious Oscar out and up onto her shoulder. 'Come and meet Tilda, the settlement's health-care worker.'

Holding a hat on Oscar's head, she marched toward what looked not much better than a corrugated-iron shed, although it had curtained louvre windows and a fly-wire door. An Aboriginal woman stepped out of the building, a large smile on her face. 'Dr Tess, you had the baby!'

Cal stood back, watching the exchange between the women, struck by the warmth on both sides.

'He's got a good set of lungs on 'im.' Tilda laughed as Oscar beat his tiny fists on Tess's shoulder.

'He needs a feed.' Tess started to move past Tilda, into the clinic.

Tilda picked up a chair, blocking the doorway. 'Too hot in here, the generator's not working so no power for the air-conditioner. Better feed him under the tree.'

Cal stepped forward, putting his arms out toward the chair. 'Let me carry that for you.'

Tilda glanced at him quickly, not making eye contact, which was the indigenous way. 'You part of Dr James's mob?'

He nodded, confused and surprised that she had noticed the similarities he and James shared. Similarities that most people missed. 'That's right. I'm James's twin, Callum.'

'He was a good doctor.' Tilda turned abruptly and walked away toward the houses.

'James came out here?' The words rolled out involuntarily as he and Tess walked into the shade of the tree. That James had been a good doctor was beyond dispute. What stunned him was that James had never mentioned visiting this place.

You didn't ask.

Tess cooed to Oscar as she sat and attached him to

her breast. He wasn't certain she'd heard him, and part of him hoped she hadn't. But the moment Oscar was quiet and feeding Tess turned to him, her expression neutral but her eyes flickering with slight censure. 'Either James or I tried to come out here once a fortnight.'

He glanced around at the primitive conditions. 'Running a clinic? Doing what?'

She sighed. 'Not nearly enough.'

The anguish in her voice touched him. 'It must get over fifty degrees Celsius out here some days. Does the generator break down often?'

'Yes, and the water supply is unreliable. At the moment this settlement is relying on bottled water as the bore's so low it's brackish and undrinkable.'

His brain started kicking over. 'So gastro is a problem?'

'Amidst myriad other health and social problems caused by overcrowded living conditions.' She tilted her head toward the houses. 'It's pretty confronting, isn't it?'

He thought of the war-torn areas he worked in and was horrified to see some links. 'I feel like I've stepped out of the country.'

Tess nodded. 'I know. It's overwhelming so I deal with it one health concern at a time. Otitis media is endemic here. It affects the kids' schooling and their ability to learn, and that means they can't engage properly in society and the workforce. Tilda's gone up to round up as many kids as she can.' She smiled at him. 'I know how you hate to sit still so I thought we could do ear checks here under the tree for an hour.'

She'd worked him out far too quickly but the indignation that usually came when people commented on his workaholic tendencies failed to surface. Instead, he found himself returning her smile as a flush of pleasure washed over him. He stood up. 'I'll get the bag.'

Tess lifted Oscar up onto her shoulder. 'Can you please grab the shade tent for Oscar? I packed that next to the bag. We can set it up so he gets the cool breeze but is protected from the sun and the flies.'

He shielded his eyes from the sun and looked down at her. 'You had this all planned, didn't you? Why didn't you tell me?'

A sheepish expression played around her eyes. 'You like the surprise element of medicine. I gave you what you enjoy.'

Her words startled him. He couldn't deny he loved the drama of high-octane medicine but he was aghast that she thought he might not have come out here had she told him the real situation. 'I would have come if you'd asked.'

Her eyes filled with understanding. 'I know you would have. You've stayed in Narranbool out of duty and you would have done this out of duty, too.' She shrugged. 'Perhaps I just wanted you to do it, enjoy it and not have it feel like duty.'

Her words burned like salt on an open wound. But what could he expect? He'd been totally open about how he disliked Narranbool. Narranbool and its small-town values had stolen his brother from him and he detested it. Unsettled, he shoved his hands in his pockets, spun on his heel and walked toward the truck.

An hour later he'd handed out more antibiotics in a shorter space of time than he could ever remember. So many of the children needed grommets, the straightforward procedure every city kid with acute ear infections received as a matter of course. At least today something had been achieved to stem the current infections, but what of the future?

Throwing antibiotics at it was a bit like putting a sticky plaster on a festering wound and it rankled that he couldn't do more.

Oscar had lain contentedly watching the shadows of the tree through his fly-wire tent and listening to the song of the cicadas, before falling asleep. Tess had examined quite a few of the children as well, sitting cross-legged under the tree, never far from Oscar.

The mood of the afternoon had been relaxed, quite the opposite of his usual fraught working conditions, and Tess had been right—he'd enjoyed himself. He refused to consider that this was a new revelation.

Yeah, right. Distracted, he glanced yet again at Tess's bent head, his gaze seeming to wander over to her after each patient. Her chic-tousled hair looked messier than ever in the light breeze and he noticed more than once the way she needed to flick her fringe out of her eyes. She looked about fifteen instead of a talented doctor in her late twenties.

He couldn't stop noticing more and more things about her. The way she tugged her ear when she was thinking, how the tip of her pink tongue peeked out between her lips when she concentrated and how well her cargo pants fitted her, outlining new post-pregnancy curves.

She looked up and caught his stare, her face breaking into a serene smile. The same smile she'd showered over him at Oscar's birth. The one that seemed to peer down into his soul and say, I know.

He instantly dropped his gaze. 'I'm done. How about you?'

'I think Jessie was my last.' She turned to Tilda.

'Any more kids?'

'No. School's closed so the rest's gone hunting. We did good, though.' The indigenous health worker gave a satisfied nod toward Callum. 'You did good too for first time.'

The unexpected and simple compliment surprised him. From someone else it would have been an insult to his skills and had him bristling. But its sincerity was clear. 'Thanks, Tilda. I'm glad I could help.'

Tess winked at him. 'He's not bad for a surgeon, is he, Tilda? Although he could have been a bit quicker.'

'Hey, I was being thorough!'

'Of course you were.' Laughing, she patted him condescendingly on the shoulder.

The musical tone of her sweet laugh demanded a response and his chest expanded as a deep, full-bodied belly laugh shook him. It was like a constricting band had been released and joy surged through him for the first time in a long time.

His left hand covered hers as his right arm snaked around her waist, bringing her in against his chest. Her heart hammered against his and he stared down into eyes alive with surprise and shimmering with something else he couldn't define.

Something that cascaded over him and became part of him.

He breathed in her scent of coconut and lime and his

arms tightened around her, soaking up her warmth, absorbing her vitality and craving her lushness. Not caring who saw him, he lowered his head, his lips seeking hers, driven totally by his need to taste her again. Taste that intoxicating mix of heady desire and need that had taunted him since their only kiss.

He needed to feel the wonder of her response—her weight against his chest, her arms around his neck and her touch in his mouth. He wanted to hear her sigh with longing as he delved into the depths of that hot, receptive mouth.

'Tilda!'

He stiffened as the fear in the unknown yelling voice vibrated in the afternoon air. A barrage of unfamiliar words followed but the fear and urgency crossed all language barriers.

Tess immediately swung out of his arms.

He almost swayed as his blood pounded hard and fast though his body, which was momentarily confused as it switched from rampant desire to the adrenaline of flight and fight. He heard the chugging sound of a wheezing exhaust and over Tess's head saw a battered ute limping toward them, with a man hanging out of the side, yelling loudly.

He swung around to Tilda and spoke, his words colliding with Tess's question. 'What's wrong?'

The indigenous health worker's face crumpled. 'Jem's been shot.'

'You go now. I'll radio the flying doctors and then I'll follow with the Lifepak and the clinic's kit.' Tess threw the large red nylon medical bag at him.

He ran toward the ute and soon reached the once red

vehicle, now brown with rust. A young man, bleeding profusely from the upper chest, lay moaning, his head resting in the lap of a teenage boy, who looked terrified. Cal spoke to him. 'I'm Callum, a doctor. What's your name?'

'Ed.'

He clambered into the back. 'What happened, Ed?'

The boy's face creased in anxiety. 'We been shooting from back here. Tim drivin' and hit a rock. Gun shot 'im.'

Cal snapped on gloves and hauled out gauze to make a pressure pack, needing to stem the flow of blood before he could do anything else. 'Jem, I'm going to help you but it might hurt.'

The injured man nodded his understanding as Cal firmly pressed the gauze into place.

Tess ran up panting and hauled herself up next to him. 'I'll leave the examination to you and I'll attach him to the monitor and insert a wide-bore IV.'

'Good move.' He was instantly struck by the fact this was the first time he'd seen her without the baby since he'd met her. It seemed strange, almost wrong, and for the first time ever in an emergency his concentration deviated for a moment. 'What about Oscar?'

Shared understanding flowed between them. 'He's asleep and Tilda's with him so we can focus on Jem.' Tess opened a swab, the sharp smell of alcohol permeating the air.

Her words reassured and centred him. He checked Jem's carotid pulse. 'Tachycardic and thready. Put up Hartmann's and the aim is to try and keep his pulse less than one hundred and twenty.' He pulled out the stethoscope around his neck. 'Jem, how's your breathing?'

'Hurts.' The single word spoke volumes.

He placed the stethoscope over Jem's upper chest, listening to air entry on both sides. It was uneven. 'Help me to sit him up.'

Tess folded Jem's arm across his chest and got Ed to hold it in place. Then she assisted Cal in raising Jem to sitting.

'This might be cold, Jem.' He sloshed the bleeding area with saline to give more visual clarity as he searched for the entry wound. 'Do we have Opsite?'

'Outer pocket, second section.' Tess tightened the tourniquet and let her fingers search for a vein. 'Sucking wound?'

'Could be. I'll seal it on three sides and create a valve effect. I'm hoping that will improve his breathing.' He pulled apart the sterile 'second skin' dressing and stuck it over the entry wound. 'Jem, Ed, what were you using? Shot pellets or a bullet?'

The injuries would be quite different. A bullet would rip through a zigzag trajectory with high-velocity damage and perhaps exit the body. Shot would scatter, causing widespread damage with less force. Either way the wound was too close to the lungs and heart for Cal's peace of mind.

Jem's voice wobbled. 'Shot.'

Who knew what the extent of the damage was? And without X-ray or ultrasound it was anyone's guess.

'IV's in, pulse still thready and BP's one hundred. I'll start him on oxygen.' Tess unwound the clear plastic tubing, her actions quick but steady as she leaned down close to their patient. 'Jem, I have to put a mask on your face, OK?' With infinite care she pulled the green elastic over his head.

Cal had a brilliant team at Frontline, one he could depend on, but he'd never shared with anyone else such synchronicity as he did with Tess.

A surge of pain rocked him. *You came close with James.*

He pushed away the dull ache of regret as his fingers explored the area around the wound. 'I can feel bubbles of air under his skin.'

Tess's head swung up. 'Surgical emphysema?'

He nodded. 'It fits in with his breathing. It's a definite pneumothorax and air is leaking into the skin.'

Tess pulled out the satellite phone. 'I'll check how far away the flying doctors are.'

'Then I need you to assist me to insert a chest tube.'

He opened the large medical backpack that Tess had brought with her from the clinic and located the local anaesthetic. He drew up the clear liquid and then exchanged the needle to a finer bore. 'Jem, I'm going to make this area numb. The needle might sting but then you will only be able to feel pressure, not pain. I have to insert a tube to help you breathe.'

Jem sagged against Ed. 'Just…fix…it…Doc.'

A flock of pink cockatoos wheeled overhead, their squawking call deafening. 'I'll do my best.' His knees burned from the ribbed floor of the ute and as he kept one eye on Jem's breathing and the other on the subcutaneous administration of the lignocaine, he realised the only difference between this and a Frontline emergency was the lack of the explosions of war.

'Cal.'

His chest tightened in a strange way at her use of his abbreviated name. Up until now she'd always addressed him as Callum. He carefully withdrew the needle and looked up to see Tess chewing her lip. 'Problem?'

She blinked twice. 'They're an hour away and he just had a run of ectopic beats.'

Hell. He had a patient with a collapsed lung, unknown internal bleeding and a stressed heart. *One step at a time, Cal.* He took a deep breath. 'Let's get the chest tube in and we'll reassess his vital signs.'

Tess opened a new set of sterile gloves for him and then passed the scalpel handle and blade. He made an incision and then carefully but with firm pressure he pushed the intercostal catheter into place. He waited to hear a 'whoosh' of air being released.

Blood trickled out instead.

'Haemothorax.' Tess stated what he knew.

Jem was bleeding into his lung. 'Right, give him IV morphine for pain and Maxalon for nausea. Start a second line for antibiotics. I'll do another set of obs.'

He hoped for more even air entry. He hoped for an improvement in heart rate. 'Is your breathing easier, Jem?'

Large eyes filled with fear stared at him over the oxygen mask. 'Still…hard…to…breathe.' Jem made a fist and pressed it to his sternum. 'Hurts bad…here.'

Cal put the stethoscope back in his ears and with Tess's help in supporting Jem he listened intently to the air entry. It was more even, despite the lower lobe of the damaged lung being filled with blood, but his patient was still short of breath.

'Pressure's dropping. BP is now ninety-five.' Tess's voice was steady but deep worry lines etched her cheeks.

Cal agreed with her. They had every reason to be extremely concerned. Jem was bleeding somewhere and, despite a chest tube, his breathing was increasingly laboured. He brought the stethoscope over Jem's heart and heard muffled soft heart sounds instead of the usual reassuring 'lub-dub'. Immediately he checked his neck. Despite low blood pressure, Jem's neck veins were distended and bulged against his dark skin.

The symptoms added up in his head, leading to an unwanted conclusion. 'Tess, I think some of the shot has penetrated the pericardium and he's in tamponade.'

Her eyes widened as the ramifications of his diagnosis hit her. 'He's got fluid crushing his heart?' Her voice rose slightly. 'And the flying doctors are still ages away.'

He was already way ahead of her. 'I'm going to have to do a pericardiocentesis, remove the fluid and hope that is enough until he can get to Theatre.' *Hope he doesn't go into cardiac arrest.*

He read his unvoiced thought on Tess's face. 'I know it's not ideal but we don't have an easy choice. If we wait he might arrest. If we do the procedure, he might arrest, but without the procedure he's only going downhill.'

He sought her eyes. 'I've done this before and with the Lifepak we have a good ECG trace. Have the ET tube and bag on hand, just in case.'

The panic in her eyes dimmed slightly and the competent doctor came back. 'You'll need a needle and a twenty-mil syringe.' She quickly located the equipment from the pack.

'Jem, mate, I'm sorry but I have to insert another needle into your chest. Ed, you hold his hand?'

Jem, now panting for breath, hardly responded and the terrified Ed immediately complied.

Longing for ultrasound guidance but dealing with reality, Cal instructed Tess. 'I want you to tell me exactly what his ECG is doing as I insert the needle.'

'Ready when you are, Mr Halroyd.'

The use of his emergency surgeon title reassured him. 'At least he doesn't have mediastinal shift.' He carefully inserted the centesis needle two centimetres below the bottom of the sternum, and two centimetres to the left of the midline, aspirating gently as he went.

'ST elevation.' Tess told him he'd gone too far into the ventricle.

Clenching his jaw, he concentrated on easing back and withdrawing the needle slightly. 'What's the rhythm like now?'

'Steadier. You're doing great.'

Blood filled the syringe. He hoped it was fluid from around the heart and not ventricular blood.

'Looking better. Normal waves.'

Relief flooded him—he was in the right place.

Tess kept up a report, being his eyes for the heart while all his concentration focused on a steady hand and the millimeter-by-millimetre needle movement.

'Ideally we'd have a three-way tap and leave this in, but we don't.' He withdrew the needle and immediately looked at the rhythm. Normal sequence. He wanted to high five Tess. 'What's his BP?'

Tess quickly pumped up the sphygmomanometer.

'Stable at one hundred and five. I'll keep up the Hartmann's.'

'It's going to be a fine line between maintaining circulating volume and heading into pulmonary oedema.' He listened to Jem's lungs again. It wasn't good. He needed surgery and he needed it now. 'Any chance the plane will be earlier than later?'

Tim, the driver of the ute, came running back from the clinic and from Tilda. 'Doc! Doc! Plane's coming. Can I drive to the airstrip?'

Callum yelled back, 'Take it slowly, mate. Crawl. I've got Jem this far and I intend to get him onto the plane.'

Fifteen minutes later they watched the plane take off in a plume of red dust. Tess reached out and gripped his hand. 'You gave Jem a fighting chance. If you hadn't been here he might not be alive.'

'You could have done this.'

She shook her head firmly. 'No. I couldn't. I'm a researcher dusting up my clinical skills as a GP, not an emergency-care specialist. James would have been the one to do it and he would have done it in the same calm and thorough way you did.' Her smile slowly rolled across her face. 'Today, for the very first time, I saw James in you, or did I see you in James?'

James. His twin. James, who had excelled in surgery, who had often beaten him in ability, and yet had thrown it all away.

Thrown away everything they'd both believed in to come to outback western New South Wales. The back of beyond and the middle of nowhere.

Except today he'd felt like he was working for Frontline. Suddenly nothing about Narranbool seemed as clear cut in his head as it always had been.

CHAPTER NINE

'I'VE got the soft towels, the nappy, a singlet and his sleeping-bag nightie, as well as cream for his bottom.' Callum's hand raked through his hair, his face tense with a frown. 'Is that everything?'

Tess used every ounce of willpower to keep a straight face and not burst out laughing. Callum Halroyd didn't hesitate when it came to plunging a needle into a man's chest to find the tiny space between the heart and lungs but he went to pieces organising a baby's bath.

She smiled up at him from where she knelt next to the bath. 'I reckon you've got all the bases covered, thanks.'

Oscar kicked his legs in the water as he floated on his back supported by Tess's arm. She loved bathtime and she gazed down at his perfect form, never ceasing to be amazed at the wonder of how this baby was a person in miniature. She tickled him with her free hand.

His dark eyes stared up at her and his mouth widened into a grin. She squealed with delight. 'Oscar just smiled at me.'

Callum dropped down next to her, excitement simmering in his grey eyes. 'Really? It's not just wind?'

'Of course it's not wind. I tickled him and he smiled.' She traced her fingers over Oscar's tummy.

Callum's shoulders brushed hers as he dropped his hands into the water and gently scooped water over the baby's legs.

His body heat swirled through her. A week ago, out at the settlement, he'd held her so close that her breasts had flattened against his chest and their hearts had hammered against each other, thundering in equal need. His arms had both corralled and cradled her at the same time, their touch unyielding yet tender, and she'd wanted to stay cocooned there for ever. His scent of musk and citrus had enveloped her as his head had dipped towards hers, and she'd tilted her lips, to his anticipating and longing for his kiss. Wanting it. Needing it like she needed air.

And then there had been the accident.

The loss of the moment had been akin to the physical pain of being winded, and she'd quickly swung out of his arms before he'd read the pain and disappointment she knew would have been etched on her face. The emergency had consumed them and now the daily routine had taken over and everything was back to normal. Well, normal for them, whatever this strange time was called when they acted like new parents but weren't.

You're not Oscar's mother. This time will end. The rational, sensible words grounded her again but not without a shard of pain.

'Do you want to hold him while I soap him?' Tess asked, hoping he would say yes. The more time Callum spent with Oscar, the better. Much as it pained her, he and his parents were Oscar's real caregivers.

'Sure.' He slid his arm behind hers, gently circling Oscar's tiny upper arm with his broad palm.

Tingling whirls of desire threatened to send her into a shaking and dizzy mess. 'Have you got him? He can be slippery.'

'All fine here. You can remove your arm.' He started chanting, 'This little piggy went to market, this little piggy stayed home,' as he tickled Oscar's feet.

Her heart turned over. Action man had a soft side that only Oscar got to see.

Oscar squealed and sent a wave of water up over the edge of the baby bath that splashed down both their fronts.

Callum laughed. 'My mind boggles at how my parents coped with twins. Look at us, we're both soaked bathing one small baby.'

She remembered her childhood—one of quick showers so the hot water didn't run out before the long line of other kids in the group home had had their turns. A childhood where she'd longed for a family and a sibling. 'What was it like, growing up as a twin?'

His hand paused in scooping water. 'It was wonderful. I had a permanent friend and ally.'

His words echoed what she'd always believed about twins but since she'd met Callum he'd hardly mentioned James, which didn't make a lot of sense. 'Did you both always want to be doctors?' She carefully rubbed Oscar's skin creases with baby soap, trying to sound conversational rather than interrogatory.

He nodded slowly, his eyes filling with memories. 'We toyed momentarily with the idea of vet science at age eight after James brought home a stray dog, but that didn't last long. Grandpa, mum's father, was a doctor and he converted us with lots of stories of blood and gore, which he knew would appeal to young boys.

'We'd play shoot-'em-up games in the back yard with water pistols and then use Mum's old sheets to bandage each other up.' His mouth twitched up on one side. 'Once we even cut our hands so we had real blood on the sheet.'

She laughed, knowing him well. 'And that would have been your idea.'

He grinned sheepishly. 'Yep, and Mum went ballistic when she found out. Her favourite expression to James was, "If he jumped off a cliff, would you follow?"'

She thought of the James she'd known, the man of firm convictions. 'But I can't imagine he would have always followed you.'

'No.' The word shot out harsh and uncompromising as all the humour on his face fled, leaving a tightness she'd occasionally glimpsed. He put his free hand under Oscar's other arm and lifted him out of the bath, straight over to the change table and into the waiting fluffy towel that had a hood to keep him warm.

The actions spoke as loudly as a tympani drum. Had she just unintentionally brushed on the reason he didn't talk about his brother? She thought about their differences, although just lately she'd been more aware of their similarities. But one big difference stood out—how he didn't love Narranbool. *I'm an ex-pat through and through.*

Then a thought came to her so clearly it almost knocked her over. 'Did you expect James to follow you to Frontline?'

The question fired into Callum with the tearing and searing accuracy of an arrow. He blocked it out by concentrating on Oscar, quickly towelling him dry and wrapping him snugly while he wrestled with the nappy and flailing legs.

A hand rested on his shoulder, the touch both firm and gentle. 'Cal?'

The softly spoken name pulled at the seal he'd rammed down on the place he'd tried to bury all his sadness and pain about James. The seal that had been fixed in place until their day at the aboriginal settlement, when it had started to crumble around the edges. He kept his head down, pinning the nappy in place.

Tess moved her hand and came around the other side of the change table, handing him a singlet. 'I worked with James for six months and shared a house with him and Carolyn for just as long. I think I knew him pretty well, if that helps.'

He'd held onto his anger and pain long past its use-by date. Now James was gone and he hated that he hadn't spoken to him more recently. He had no one to blame but himself—the fault lay squarely at his feet. James had tried to contact him a few times but because he hadn't responded, had stopped.

Tess's warm eyes roved over him, encouraging and supportive. He doubted whether telling her would help him but, hell, keeping it all locked inside him hadn't helped either. He pulled Oscar's nightie over his head and snapped the bottom of it shut, so he was snug and toasty for the night.

Scooping him up, he breathed in the scent of baby— soap, sunshine and milk—and handed him to Tess for a feed. He tossed the towels in the basket and walked toward the door, pausing at the threshold. 'Come on, this story will go down better over a glass of wine.'

She gave him her serene smile. 'That sounds like a good idea.'

He nodded curtly, and walked to the kitchen to open a bottle of Mudgee red, already regretting his decision to talk about James.

Tess walked into the lounge room and settled herself on the couch, her legs tucked up under her and Oscar contentedly sucking at her breast.

The image socked him in his chest and his hand slipped on the waiter's friend, the cork coming out at a rakish angle. His hand trembled as he poured the wine. Setting down the bottle, he took in a deep breath. He had a job to go back to and so did she. All this domestic cosiness was just temporary. It would finish soon.

He carried the glasses over and took a long sip of the heavy wine, savouring the flavours of liquorice and raspberry, enjoying the punch of the tannins. He raised his glass. 'To James. He loved this wine.'

'To James.' Tess took a small sip and placed the glass on the side table, before turning back to rest her inquisitive gaze on him.

He sat down. 'I guess I start at the beginning. James and I did everything together from as long as I can remember, and when we qualified, we entered the surgery programme. We'd made a pact to work in overseas aid.'

He heard her gasp of surprise. *Thanks, bro*. So James had kept his own counsel and asked Carolyn to keep it as well—their falling-out hadn't gone beyond themselves.

She stroked Oscar's head. 'I knew he had skills above those of a city GP but country medicine demands more. How far into the programme did he get?'

Cal dragged his eyes from the hypnotic effect of Tess's fingers and concentrated on answering her question. 'Pretty far. And then just as everything was firming up for Frontline and Felicity and I were falling apart, James announced that he and Carolyn were moving up here.' He heard his voice rise, heard the old anger, the sense of bewilderment, and he stood up, needing to pace.

Perception shone in the depths of her warm eyes. 'I imagine it must have come completely out of left field.'

'I couldn't believe it.' He thumped his right fist into his left palm. 'He'd deviated from his lifelong plan!'

Tess started as Oscar pulled off the breast, turning his head toward the noise. 'Or had he deviated from *your* lifelong plan?'

His anger tossed off the quietly spoken voice of reason. 'That's semantics. We had a plan. We'd had this plan since…for ever, and he changed it without any consultation.' He raked his hair with his hand. 'Hell, he had amazing skills, skills the world needed, and he tossed them away to bury himself here.' He threw out his arms in derision at all that surrounded him.

Tess resettled Oscar, her shoulders tense. 'You really believe that?'

Visions of the day at the settlement flashed through his mind but chagrin surged through him, burying them. 'Of course I do. Narranbool Hospital is hardly a world-class facility and you evacuate every serious case.'

She fixed him with a long look. 'So do you at Frontline. You patch and despatch.'

'It's a war zone!' Why had he tried to explain? No one understood. 'James would have saved more lives working for Frontline than he would have here.'

Tess's plump lips folded inwards for a moment. 'If Narranbool hadn't had a doctor last week, Ruth would have died.'

'She's eighty-five!' The words came out on a wave of frustration.

'With a mind as sharp as a tack and a family who adore her.' Tess stood up and tucked Oscar into the bassinet that moved from room to room. She turned back, her arms folded across her chest. 'And what about Jem and Vince?'

He shrugged. 'OK, so sometimes things get hairy in Narranbool, but mostly it's not like that. I know, I've spent just over two weeks basically writing prescriptions. Narranbool didn't need a surgeon of James's calibre to be their doctor. The people of a warring nation did.'

She stood by the window with the fire-red light of the setting sun making a halo of colour above her honey-blonde hair. She looked ethereal. 'I think you needed him the most.'

Her precise words rained down on him, cleaving at the seal, releasing the pent-up pain, allowing it to well up and tighten his chest and throat. 'That's ridiculous.'

She walked toward him. 'Is it?' Her arm touched his. 'I don't have any siblings but I can only imagine what it must have been like to have been on the same wavelength for so long and then to have different wants and needs. It must have felt like everything you believed in had been ripped out from under you. Like you'd lost half of yourself.'

Her words so accurately depicted how he felt that they scared him. It was like waking up naked and surrounded by a thousand pairs of eyes, and he hated feeling that exposed. The house suddenly seemed small and claustrophobic and he needed to get out into the evening air. Needed to clear his head.

He stepped away from Tess, forced himself away from her touch that he craved so much, and headed to the door. 'We're out of milk. I'll be back soon.' He didn't need anyone feeling sorry for him, but as he closed the door behind him he couldn't shut out Tess's compassionate look.

His blood pumped through him, a red tide of anger, and he moved quickly, pounding the pavement. He intended to walk the kilometre out to the highway and buy milk at the roadhouse, knowing that none of the shops in town would be open at this time of night. The place shut down like a drum at five o'clock except for the pub and Friday-night shopping.

Long shadows cast by the flowering eucalypts patterned the road as he made his way along two residential streets before turning up toward the intersection. A few people were out walking their dogs, embracing the cooler autumn evenings.

'Evening, Doctor, lovely night for it. How's the little chap doing?' Gerry Gibson instructed his golden retriever to sit and then leaned against a fence, awaiting a reply.

Cal smiled. He'd given up expecting to be called 'Mr' here. As far as the locals were concerned, he was a doctor so that was what he would be called. 'Oscar's doing very well, thank you, and growing so much every day.'

Gerry grunted. 'They do that, and nothing stops them.' He scratched the dog's ears. 'We've been pretty worried about Ralph Denton, and I caught up with him the other day. He's the best I've seen him since Edna died—said he'd had a chat with you.' Gerry slapped him on the arm in a friendly gesture. 'Don't know what you said but it did the trick.'

Cal had experienced a heavy stream of patients through the surgery every day but he remembered Ralph because he hadn't been able to solve the problem with the prescription pad. 'I don't think I did much except listen.'

The veranda light of the house they stood in front of lit up, its light bright and white. 'Is that you, Gerry?' a woman's voice enquired.

'That's right, Betty. Just talking out here to the doc.'

Heels sounded on the wooden steps and then a middle-aged woman came down the path to the gate, clutching an egg carton. 'Oh, Dr Callum, I'm so glad you're here.' She pushed the eggs toward him. 'I thought you might enjoy some free-range eggs as a little thank you. You were so wonderful with Mum the other night, especially as she was so upset about poor Dr James.'

Betty dropped her voice conspiratorially. 'She can be a bit cantankerous when she's sick, but you wrapped her around your handsome finger and she's being really good with her medication now.'

Mavis Cooper had experienced bouncing blood-sugar levels. Once again he'd really only listened and then reviewed her medications and glucometer technique. He accepted the eggs with a smile. 'It was my pleasure.'

The words came out as an automatic response but he was surprised by the sense of well-being that followed. Neither of these two consultations with patients came close to the seat-of-the-pants medicine he practised every day with Frontline. There he saved lives with brilliant technical skills that defied the odds. It was impossible to compare that with the little he'd done for Ralph and Mavis.

'Well, we'd better let you go. You're a busy man.' Betty bustled back through the gate.

Cal bade them goodnight and walked away, hearing Betty ask Gerry how his wife's latest quilt was coming along. He kept walking and met half a dozen more people on his journey, all of them pausing to chat, all asking about Oscar and many wishing to squeeze his hand firmly as they offered condolences about James.

This walk was supposed to have cleared his head but instead his mind whirled. The care and concern of the townsfolk both settled and unsettled him, and his life in a war zone two and a half weeks ago seemed a lifetime away.

An uncomplicated lifetime ago where there were only two settings—life or death. A time before he'd met Tess. Tess, who stirred up feelings he didn't want to examine. A time before Oscar and his nephew's total dependence on him. A time when his mother had been an indomitable strength.

The pull of family, work and a pair of warm brown eyes tugged him in different directions.

But life on the frontline was where he belonged, where his skills were best used for the greater good. He knew he could continue his important work and still be a loving uncle for Oscar.

As he walked up the path toward the front door he could see Tess's silhouette through the window. Oscar lay on her shoulder fast asleep as she patted him firmly with her hand and swayed back and forth to an imaginary beat. The vision slugged him with wonder, joy and a general sense of unease. As his key hit the lock he realised he'd completely forgotten to buy the milk.

'I've got good news!' Callum's rich voice sounded from the garden.

Tess turned from the computer where she'd been reading yet another email from London, asking her what her intentions were in regard to her job. They wanted an answer as soon as possible and she continued to prevaricate. Sooner rather than later she had to have the *big* conversation with Cal and his parents.

Callum stepped through the French doors from the garden with Oscar on his chest, snuggled up in the baby sling. 'Did you hear? I have great news.'

She laughed as his enthusiasm surrounded her. 'A moment ago it was good news and now it's great news. Pretty soon it will be excellent.' She stood up and plugged in the kettle, keeping her gaze on him, soaking up the sight of him while she could, storing him in her memory. The wind had ruffled his hair and her action man looked unusually relaxed. *Your action man?* She tossed her head to silence the voice. 'So, what's your news?'

A beaming smile raced across his face, stripping away the anguish that had hovered there last night when he'd talked about James. 'Dr Leo Turnington just called and he's driving from Mildura as we speak. He'll be here in a couple of hours and starts work tomorrow with a view of buying the practice.'

Her stomach sank and her hands stilled on the tea caddy. She'd thought she had another week before her make-believe family ended. Before she had to make some big decisions, before she had to say goodbye to this domestic trio with Callum and Oscar. 'That's great.' Could he hear how false her voice sounded?

'Yeah, it is, isn't it?'

He grabbed her around the waist, his fingers gently pressing into her skin and the heat of his palm sending a jolt of desire spiralling through her, leaving her quivering in its wake. He twirled her around the kitchen in a quick two-step, with Oscar between them, making her breathless and wanting more.

He grinned. 'And it gets better.'

That probably means it's worse for me. She stared up into clear grey eyes that shone with relief and excitement, a confusing combination. 'Does it?'

'It does. Mum's doing really well but she's driving Dad mad in Melbourne so they've got permission from her doctor and Dad's taking her to Roseport. They've got a holiday house there and the change of scenery will do them both good. They're always more relaxed at the coast.'

She tried to steady her hammering heart. 'It's great that your mum's improving so quickly.' And she meant it. Jennifer deserved good health but her improvement meant she was getting closer to being able to care for Oscar. It meant her own role was winding back.

Cal nodded, his body almost vibrating with exhilaration. 'I thought now that Leo is here and Narranbool is sorted for a doctor, we'd go as well.'

Her breath swooped out of her lungs and her blood rushed to her feet, making her sway. So this was it. She'd thought she had another week before the locum she'd arranged arrived, but everything had just changed. Callum and Oscar were leaving Narranbool.

She reached out and touched the downy softness of Oscar's head. 'When…?' She dragged in a fortifying breath. 'When do you and Oscar leave?'

His high brow creased in a frown as unaccustomed confusion settled over his take-charge demeanour. His fingers gently brushed her fringe out of her eyes. 'Not just Oscar and me—you too, the three of us. We can't go without you.'

The three of us. His words wrapped around her like a cloak on a cold night, warm, cosy and comforting. He wanted her to go with them. But her brain struggled to work out what he meant, having swung from the idea of Callum and Oscar leaving to her leaving with Callum and Oscar. Dizzy and perplexed, she sought confirmation. 'You can't?'

'Of course we can't. I want you to come with us.'

Joy whirled through her so fast the kitchen seemed to spin. He wanted her. She heard his voice talking but the words had trouble penetrating her euphoria. She forced herself to listen.

'It will be great. The house has the most spectacular view over the ocean and the town has The Provedore, which sells the best coffee you've ever tasted. Oscar will sleep, exhausted from all that sea air, and we can sleep in.'

Memories of being snuggled up next to him, his body cradling hers, welled up inside her, sending heat and lust into every fibre. Her brain took a sharp left away from that thought and landed on 'Oscar will sleep'. She shook her head and rolled her eyes. 'In your dreams. If he sleeps through the night before six weeks, it would be a miracle. It would be a miracle if he did it at six weeks.'

He winked at her. 'Hey, a guy can hope.' He dropped a quick kiss onto the top of her head and stepped away. 'Where's that notebook?'

The soft caress of his lips on top of everything else that had happened in the last five minutes derailed all coherent thought but she could see the brightly coloured book that James had always used tucked behind the Narranbool Trivia Champion trophy. Silently, she handed it to him.

'Thanks.' With a quick and firm click he activated his pen and started scribbling down his action plan. Energy vibrated off him and as each stream of thought came to an end he'd glance up and grin before the next wave struck him.

Had she ever been that driven, known so clearly what she wanted?

You know now.

But knowing and having were two different things. She blocked out his bone-melting smile, hugged to her heart the fact he wanted her to come, and hauled her mind back to practicalities. 'It's a long drive with a baby.'

'Dad's promised the helicopter.' A dimple appeared in his cheek. 'There are *some* perks in being a Halroyd. I'm so glad things are going to finish this way.'

The word hung there like a prickly cactus she didn't want to touch. 'Finish?'

He nodded as he scrawled down another few words on his list. 'Dad and I both thought it was an ideal situation for everyone. We can have a couple of weeks of having a holiday and slowly transfer over Oscar's care. You know, get him used to a bottle, slowly wean him from you and introduce him to Mum, Dad and the nanny. Plus, it will give you a real rest before you head to London and a way for us to say thanks.'

An icy chill froze the blood in her veins. She'd had almost three weeks and this was the beginning of the end. She was the surrogate and her role had been extended to help, but now as it ceased to be needed it was being curtailed with Halroyd efficiency.

Part of her wanted to refuse to go to Roseport. Part of her wanted to throw his offer of a holiday back in his face. Why go and prolong the pain?

But she couldn't do that to Oscar. Callum was right, there needed to be a period of transfer of care. She owed that to Oscar and to Carolyn and James.

And, so help her, if she was totally honest, she'd sell her soul to spend precious final hours with Callum. She plastered a bright smile on her face. 'I'll go and pack.'

CHAPTER TEN

THE old wooden boathouse with its new blue colour-bond roof sat perched on its weathered stilts, staking a claim on a tiny patch of yellow sand, like a grand Victorian dame. Tess stood on its tiny deck and scanned the bay. Callum had taken the powerboat and headed to the main pier to buy mussels.

It was the end of a wonderful Roseport day and Tess had enjoyed crewing for Patrick on the small yacht James and Callum had used when they'd been children. As they'd sailed around the bay she'd listened with increasing delight to the many stories Patrick had told her about the twins' summer exploits. Most of them had involved a 'brilliant' idea of Callum's with a variety of consequences ranging from a broken leg to a sea rescue.

It was hard to believe that almost a week had passed since leaving Narranbool. They'd slipped easily into a routine and each morning after Oscar's early feed she and Cal would jog down to the corner shop to buy the papers. Then they would cook the household breakfast from the fabulous selection of food in the enormous stainless-steel fridge. The days rolled out in a leisurely fashion but always finished the same way—bathing Oscar together.

Tess had expected Oscar's nanny to be in Roseport when they arrived but Jennifer and Patrick were the only other occupants of the house and the nanny had not been mentioned. Tess had no plans to bring the subject up. Right now she was cocooning herself in a fantasy-land of family life and until she was hauled out of it she had no plans to face reality and depart.

'Ahoy, Tess.' Cal gave her a mock salute as he passed the dock and then threw her a line.

She caught it and quickly wrapped it around the bollard as Cal put the engine into reverse and steered the craft into position, parallel to the dock. Like everything he did, he did it with precision, skill and a dash of charm. She could watch him for ever.

He cut the engine and jumped out of the boat with the ease of a seasoned sailor. 'Where's Oscar?'

'Your parents took him up to the house. They wanted a turn at bathing him and giving him some expressed breast milk.'

Cal gave her an unexpected look. 'You OK?'

'Fine.' She'd thought she'd sounded upbeat rather than down, which was closer to the truth, but she had no right to deny Oscar's grandparents time with their grandson.

He slung his arm casually around her shoulder like he often did, his touch friendly yet slightly proprietorial as he gently pulled her into his side and turned her round to face the setting sun.

'Well, that's lucky really.'

She raised her face to his, enjoying the way the final fiery red rays lit up his hair. 'How so?'

'They'd sold out of mussels.'

She pretended to pout and tapped his chest with her finger. 'The mussels you spent all day raving about, the mussels you told me I hadn't really lived if I hadn't tasted them, the mussels you *promised* me.'

He grinned sheepishly. 'That'd be the ones, yeah. But…' He dropped his arm and knelt down on the edge of the dock, reaching into the boat and pulling out a bottle of champagne and a polystyrene box. 'The cray boat had this baby here, but it's not big enough for four.' He stood up, devilment dancing in his eyes. 'I guess we'll just have to stay down here and eat it.'

Lightness shimmered through her. 'I suppose that would only be good manners.'

He walked into the boathouse, down to the old wide, saggy couches and the small kitchen area. 'My mother is very big on manners.'

Tess followed, smiling. 'I wouldn't want to offend Jennifer.' She pulled out some plates and glasses from the old meat safe which was now used as a cupboard.

She turned round as Cal pulled the cork out of the bottle with a loud 'pop'. Foam cascaded up over the neck of the bottle and she quickly put a glass underneath it, catching the straw-coloured contents.

He poured the second glass and put the bottle down. Stepping in close, he tilted his glass to hers. 'To a great day.'

She stared up at him, into the warmth of his eyes, and spoke the truth. 'To the most momentous few weeks of my life.'

He nodded slowly. 'It's had everything, hasn't it? Death, life, no sleep, emergencies, monotony, tears and laughter all packed into four short weeks.' He stared down at her, and then without breaking eye contact he slowly took her glass out of her hands and placed it, along with his, next to the bottle.

Raising his hands, he cupped her cheeks in his palms and leaned his forehead against hers. 'And through it all you've been totally amazing. Caring, giving, gorgeous and completely sexy.'

She wanted to fling her head back and scream with delight. He wanted her as much as she wanted him. 'Me? Sexy?'

'Oh God, yes.' The words came out on a moan and he lowered his lips to hers and kissed her.

Gone was the hesitancy of his previous kiss. Gone was the gentle tracing of his lips on hers in tentative exploration. This time his kiss claimed her mouth hard and fast with all the determined finesse of a man who knew what he wanted and wasn't afraid to ask for it.

And she met him stroke for stroke, thrust for thrust as their tongues danced together in a journey of unmet need. Tasting, touching, taking, giving, wanting, needing. All of it miraculous, none of it enough.

Without breaking contact with his wondrous lips, she wound her arms around his neck and trailed her fingers through his thick, soft hair, as she'd longed to do since the moment she'd met him.

He dropped his hands from her face and pulled her against him, closing all tiny gaps until their bodies moulded together like two pieces of a puzzle. His heart hammered hard against her breasts and with a groan he slid his mouth from her lips and trailed kisses along her jaw, down into the hollow of her neck.

She'd never known anything like it. All the days spent gazing at him, talking with him and parenting with him had culminated in tinder-dry desire and it only took one look, one touch and one taste to ignite it. Her head dropped back as each kiss blasted a trail of pleasure through her, burning her skin with a raging need that vaporised all thought. Her hands reached under his T-shirt, her fingers tingling to touch all that golden skin stretched taut over hard, toned muscle.

'Your scent has driven me crazy from the first time I met you.' His voice sounded thick and unsteady as he pulled away slightly and tugged his shirt over his head, letting it drop to the floor. 'You smell divine, like fresh fruit.'

She ran her fingers through the lock of hair that fell against his forehead, thrilled that he had been as tormented by her as she had by him. She'd never wanted anyone as much as she wanted him right now. Wrapping her free arm around his waist, she tugged him forward. 'Feel free to taste me.'

His eyes darkened to a shimmering black but he hesitated for a moment. 'Are you sure?'

There were so many things in her life right now that she wasn't sure about. She wasn't sure about which job to take or her role in Oscar's life, but making love with Callum was the *one* thing she was clear about. Crystal clear. Pulling her blouse over her head, she lifted her mouth to his. 'I've never been more sure about anything.'

Cal's self-restraint shattered at her words. For weeks his waking thoughts and dreams had been filled with this incredible woman. How her early morning husky voice made him go hard at 'hello', how delicious she smelt after she stepped out of the shower, and how her lush mouth closed so seductively around a strawberry at breakfast.

With every passing day he'd wanted her more and more, but her body had just been through a rite of passage. 'We'll take it slowly.'

She smiled that knowing smile. 'Or not.' Her hands closed over the waistband of his board shorts and tugged.

White lights danced in his head. With a flick of his right hand he reached around and unclasped her bra. Her breasts, full and heavy, tumbled free and he stared in awe as if seeing them for the first time. Seeing them exclusively for himself. His arms circled her and he lowered her onto the old couch, regret tugging him. 'It should be a comfortable bed.'

She shook her head and traced her finger along his lips. 'I love it here.'

'So do I.' He buried his head in her neck and with the tang of salt in the air and the sound of lapping waves he explored her body, stroking and tasting every part, branding her with his touch and making her moan with the complicated connection of bliss and pain until he couldn't hold back any longer.

With her hands frantically clutching him and her legs wrapped tightly around his waist, he eased himself slowly inside her, marvelling at how her body opened, drawing him in as if he was coming home.

'Now, Cal. Please, now.'

Her strangled voice called to him, driving him forward until he heard her cry out. Then he joined her, spiralling out with her, far, far away, momentarily released from all the demands and duty that normally anchored him so firmly to the ground.

Tess lay under a scratchy blanket on a lumpy old couch and it was the most wonderful place she'd ever known. Cal's arms encircled her, his breath tickled her neck and one of his legs was tucked between hers, its pressure firm on the place that tingled and shimmered every time she thought of him.

Making love had been so unexpected and yet so natural—an extension of everything they'd shared over the last month. They'd lived together, worked together and parented together. Coming together now had been the final connection. The ultimate bond.

She breathed in deeply and stroked the arms that cherished her, knowing that she had never in her life experienced such contentment. This was what life was all about.

Real life.

Her fog of euphoria instantly evaporated as real life hammered hard on the gates of her fantasy world. Life was about family and this thing right now wasn't anything to do with that.

But we just made love.

No, that was lust and sex.

Her heart stalled as she saw it for what it really was. Cal had just had sex but she'd fallen in love.

No! No! No!

Yes. Fallen in love with a man whose focus was far removed from the idea of a nuclear family and firmly centred thousands of miles away.

She bit her lip to stop herself from crying out as pain lanced her.

'You OK?' Cal's finger stroked down her cheek.

'Fine.' The lie was so much easier than the truth.

'We've got just over a week before you leave for London. Let's make the most of it.' He nibbled her ear as his fingers found her breast.

Desire flooded her, derailing her thoughts and stirring unsated need into whirling demand. Accepting she was both weak and pathetic for not dealing with her future, and for hiding behind a make-believe reality, she kissed him and gave herself up to short-term bliss.

Tess stood barefoot on the spongy buffalo grass, gazing out over Roseport Bay and the majestic white lighthouse that guarded the entrance. The glorious autumn weather had continued—golden sunshine during the day for beach play but nippy evenings that gave the perfect excuse to light the open fire.

She turned back toward the house that had given her such a wonderful week. Tess had fallen in love with Westwinds the moment they'd arrived. Built from local sandstone at the turn of the century it had been described by the local paper of the day as a 'villa'. It oozed old-world elegance with its bay windows, its multi-layered roofline dotted with six chimneys, and welcoming large verandas, complete with gingerbread latticework. All the woodwork was pristine white, which gave the house a fresh look against the creamy gold of the large sandstone bricks.

The extensive gardens with salt-hardy plants protecting the more English-style trees had so many nooks and crannies she could imagine squealing and delighted children playing hide and seek or enjoying a wonderful Easter-egg hunt—the front lawn being *the* perfect place to see the sunrise on Easter Sunday.

Stop it, this isn't yours to attach traditions to.

She dropped her head into her hands as despair whizzed around her. She'd fallen in love with the house, the son, the baby, and the parents. The whole Halroyd package—the family she'd never had.

It was a complete and utter disaster.

Hearing crunching gravel on the path behind her, she swung round. Jennifer walked toward her, holding a trowel and wearing the most battered straw hat Tess had ever seen.

Cal's mother had benefited from the sea air and her energy level grew every day. She spent most mornings in the garden, despite the fact Patrick employed two full-time gardeners.

'I thought you were supposed to be off doing something for yourself.' Ocean-blue eyes, the same colour and intensity as James's appraised her.

Callum was holed up in the office, dealing with lawyers and executive matters, and half an hour ago Patrick and the new nanny had strapped Oscar into the 'three-wheel-all-terrain' pram and had walked into Roseport to buy the papers and bait. Tess wanted to hate the nanny but Vanessa was a delightful young woman and had fitted quickly into the family.

But her arrival meant the clock was very much ticking down and Tess was running out of time. She crossed her arms and tried not to sound defensive. 'I am doing something. I'm taking a walk in your lovely garden.'

'Come and have some tea in the l'orangerie.' Jennifer linked her arm through Tess's as they walked toward the amazing glass structure at the back of the house that caught the sunshine and the stunning views. 'I remember my mother coming over when the twins were three weeks old and shooing me out of the house.' She smiled at the recollection. 'I thought I would love being able to go shopping for an hour all on my own, but I spent most of the time wondering how the boys were.'

She patted Tess's hand in understanding as they stepped onto the white marble floor of the l'orangerie and sat down at a table set with scones, jam and cream and a steaming pot of tea. 'For four weeks your life has revolved around little Oscar and now, with a bit of time off, you don't quite know what to do with yourself.'

Tess nodded. 'But you came home to your boys.'

Jennifer placed the tea strainer over the cup and lifted up the teapot. 'I did, and Oscar will be back soon, too.'

Her throat tightened. 'But one day very soon he won't be coming back to me.'

'Callum says you're going to work in London.' The older woman passed the cup of tea and offered Tess the plate of scones as if she hadn't heard the emotional crack in Tess's voice.

London, Narranbool, she had no idea. 'I'm not certain what I'm doing.'

Surprise crossed Oscar's grandmother's face. 'Oh. Cal seemed very sure of your plans.'

Tess picked up a scone and broke it in half. 'Cal assumed.'

'Yes, he does have a habit of doing that, dear.' She

gave Tess a knowing look. 'I love him dearly and he's blessed with amazing talent, drive and determination, but he forgets that not everyone is as focused as him and, more importantly, that not everyone wants what he wants.' She sighed. 'Although I thought he might have learned by now.'

A jolt of surprise shot through Tess and she suddenly felt like she had an ally in Jennifer. 'You know about his falling-out with James?'

'Mothers know more than their children ever give them credit for. We knew something was amiss and we filled in the gaps.' She stirred her tea thoughtfully. 'It was an incredibly selfless gift to give Oscar life and make James and Carolyn parents.' She levelled her gaze at Tess with the accuracy of a gun-sight. 'Exactly what was your plan before their…before the accident?'

Normally, Tess would have felt that she'd been put on the spot, but instead she welcomed the chance to talk with someone who might just understand. 'At the start of the pregnancy I thought I'd go to London as planned. I don't have any family, no ties, and I've always worked wherever the job has taken me.'

She spread a generous amount of the home-made raspberry jam onto the buttery scone. 'But just before the accident I was leaning toward committing to life in Narranbool. Taking up James's offer of joining him in the practice, buying a house close by and being an honorary auntie to Oscar.'

'You lost family, too.'

Jennifer's sympathetic gaze threatened to bring Tess to tears. 'I did, and now I feel like I'm drifting.'

Jennifer cleared her throat. 'Given we can't bring

James and Carolyn back…but what if I could wave a magic wand? What would you ask for?'

Her words rushed out, straight from her heart. 'I want Oscar.'

Jennifer stiffened, shock lining her face, fear flitting across her eyes. 'Want him?'

Tess reached out and touched her hand. 'I don't mean I want to take him from you. I would never take him from his loving family. I grew up without a family and I would never wish that on a child.'

Jennifer relaxed and squeezed her hand. 'So what do you really mean when you say you want Oscar?'

She bit her lip and took a deep breath. 'I feel like I'm his mother and I want to be part of his life. I want to share his care with you and Vanessa, be a part of the team that raises him. I want to be there to see him take his first steps, take him to the park, build sandcastles with him, and be a real presence in his life.'

Jennifer smiled and nodded. 'My dear, I hoped that was going to be your wish. Does that make things more certain for you?'

Like a heavy weight being lifted from her shoulders, she felt intense clarity and lightness. All her life she'd sat back and waited. Waited to be adopted by a family. Waited for Curtis to finish medicine. She was done waiting. Now she knew exactly what she wanted and how she had to fight to get it.

CHAPTER ELEVEN

'I HAVE to agree, this is *the* best coffee I've ever tasted.'

Cal glanced up from checking the football scores and grinned at Tess. She sat sipping her frothy latte at the table outside The Provodore on Roseport's main street. Oscar lay in his pram between them, soporific with milk and staring dazedly up at the string of bright toys Cal had just bought him at the toyshop.

Leaning forward, he gently pressed his thumb against her top lip and swiped it across her skin, loving the soft silky touch. 'You look like Oscar, with a milk moustache.'

She laughed, the tinkling sound heating his blood. 'Well, we both know what we enjoy, don't we, buddy?' She tickled Oscar's feet.

Since the night they'd first made love, his need to touch her had increased tenfold and he'd found himself brushing his hand against her neck as she stood on the deck watching the sun set, unable to resist lightly squeezing her buttock as she leaned into the fridge while they prepared breakfast, and stealing a kiss when he knew his parents and the nanny were not around. He didn't need his parents knowing that he and Tess were having a holiday fling. He had enough to organise in a few short days without questioning looks.

In fact, he should be in the office right now but it had rained all day yesterday and he hadn't been able to get out and exercise. He'd woken up that morning to sunshine and a burning need to spend time with Tess and Oscar. He'd suggested that they walk into town despite the fact that according to his carefully devised timetable, the nanny was to be on deck for the morning so he and Tess could make their personal final arrangements for heading back to their respective jobs.

The main street was buzzing—everyone else in Roseport embracing the chance to shed themselves of cabin fever. People wandered past—enthusiastic joggers, Lycra-clad cyclists, elderly citizens chatting to everyone as they walked their dogs, and just behind him he could hear a family negotiating over which cake they would buy to take home.

People smiled at him as they passed. Smiled the smile that a new baby generated either from fond memories of the past or hopeful anticipation of the future. Callum prickled with a combination of pride and unease.

'Cal Halroyd? Is that you?'

He recognised the voice of the father who'd been moderating the debate between his children about the cake and he swung round.

A tall red-haired man strode towards him. 'I thought you were overseas?' Turquoise-green eyes took in Tess and Oscar. 'But here you are with a gorgeous wife and baby.'

Cal quickly covered the streak of horror that ripped through him at the misunderstanding by standing up and warmly shaking the man's hand. 'Alex, good to see you.' He turned toward Tess, whose usual open and smiling expression was suddenly closed. 'Alex is Roseport's GP. Alex Fitzwilliam, this is Dr Tess Dalton and my nephew, Oscar.'

'Your nephew?' Alex's look as he realised his social faux pas collided with confusion. 'I'm so sorry, I didn't realise. I met your parents the other day at the surgery and they talked about their new grandson so when I saw the three of you together…' He extended his hand to Tess. 'I do apologise.'

'Please, don't be distressed. It was a perfectly natural assumption to make—we do look like a family.' Tess shook Alex's hand and showered him with a smile that sent a jagged green light through Cal.

He didn't want to go through this in the main street and air the Halroyds' personal business. 'It's all a bit complicated.' The words came out far more brusquely than he'd intended and he ran a hand through his hair. 'How about you bring Jess and the kids up to the house for a barbecue tomorrow and a hit of tennis? We'll explain it all then.' He extended his arm casually in an arc. 'This is a bit too public.'

Alex nodded, understanding dawning in his eyes. 'Yes, of course, your parents don't need any more press attention. And we'd love to come. Woody's got pretty good at tennis and the twins love being ball-girl and -boy so Jess and I might actually have a chance at beating you this time.' He turned back to Tess. 'Lovely to meet you.'

'And you.'

Silently they both watched him walk back to his children who had finally agreed on a chocolate cake.

Cal gulped the last of his coffee and threw some coins on the table to cover the tab. 'Sorry about that.' He unlocked the pram wheels and manoeuvred the pram around the surrounding chairs.

Tess slowly picked up her jacket and silently followed him. As they left the main street and headed up Hill Road back toward Westwinds he had a strong urge to try and explain his behaviour. 'We don't know many of the locals except the Fitzwilliams and I hadn't expected to meet Alex on a weekday.' He winked, trying to soften the tension that surrounded Tess. 'Damn doctors and their easy hours.'

She levelled her gaze at him. 'Was it so awful that he mistook us for a family?'

Her quiet words hailed down on him with unerring accuracy. He deflected them. 'It's nothing to do with awful, Tess. The fact is we're not a family.'

She walked next to him. 'Not in the traditional sense, no.'

A shot of adrenaline poured through him and his heart beat faster. 'Not in any sense.'

He caught the flinch of her body and hated himself. The crunch of the pram wheels on the gravel road filled the silence between them as loudly as amplified bass at a heavy metal concert. 'I've got a tour of duty with Frontline and in two days you're heading to London.'

She stared straight ahead. 'No, I'm not.'

'What?' His stomach went into freefall. 'I don't understand. We discussed this.'

'No, we didn't.' Her voice had developed an edge. 'You *told* me I was going back to my job in London and I didn't correct you because at the time I didn't know what I was doing. By my definition, that falls a long way short of a discussion.'

He gripped the handle of the pram as memories of a conversation with James came rushing back. 'Don't tell me you're staying in Narranbool? That bloody town.'

Strands of honey-blonde hair became airborne as she quickly turned her head to face him. 'There is *nothing* wrong with Narranbool. Stop displacing your grief onto that wonderful town. I'm really sorry that you and James fell out but he had the right to choose his own path. Just because it didn't match your plans didn't make it wrong.'

Her words acted like pebbles breaking the surface of his anguish. He gritted his teeth. 'He settled.'

'No, he committed. He committed to a town and its people, to a woman he loved and to their dream of a family.'

Cal hated hearing that, hated the way it sounded almost reasonable. 'People like us, Tess, have a duty of care. We have skills that should be out there where they are needed most. I won't let you give up a promising career by burying yourself in Narranbool.'

'It's not up to you.' Her eyes flashed with a fire he'd not seen before. 'But just so you know, I won't be working in Narranbool.'

Relief surged through him. 'So you're going back into research but not in London?'

She paused at the white iron gate supported by its cap-point topped posts. 'My duty of care is to Oscar, and I'm going to work in Melbourne to be close by.'

Complete bewilderment swamped him. 'I don't understand. That's not what you planned or wanted.'

'It's not exactly what I want, no.' She gave him a look filled with pitying compassion, as if he was completely clueless. 'Callum, life isn't static. What I wanted a year ago is different from what I wanted five weeks ago and is totally different from what I want today.'

She reached out and rested her hands on his forearms, her touch eliciting the same surge of arousal he experienced every single time. But this time it was tinged with something akin to panicked alert.

She bit her lip. 'What I want and what I need is standing right in front of me. I want us. You, Oscar and me. A family.'

Her voice stroked him, her eyes implored him. Snapshots of moments they'd shared projected through his mind—laughing together as they learned how to set up the port-a-cot, arguing good-naturedly about the car seat, falling asleep together, exhausted, at four a.m. when Oscar finally stopped crying.

She stepped into his arms. 'We've been a family for five weeks and we can be a family well into the future. I love you and I want to marry you.'

Blood pounded through him, loud in his ears, and vibrating his chest. He hadn't expected a proposal.

Callum, you have to settle down one day—why not now? Felicity's voice surged forward, obliterating everything. Felicity, who had taken over his life, organised him and expected him to fall in line with all of her plans. Now Tess and Oscar were doing the same thing.

He and Flick had ended acrimoniously and he wasn't

going to live with that sort of guilt again. Every cell in his body screamed to run.

Tess held her breath, watching Cal's eyes move from light grey to stormy black. She felt him stiffen in her arms and when he stepped back from her the pain sucked the breath from her lungs.

'Tess, I'm sorry but I can't marry you.'

His words backed up his actions but she'd come this far, exposed her heart and soul, and she wasn't going down without a fight. 'Why not?'

He ground his right thumb into the palm of his left hand. 'These last few weeks have been wonderful, but not real. It's all happened so fast. Hell, six weeks ago we'd never even met and neither of us had plans to be parents'.

She tried to smile. 'And yet it worked.'

A flicker of something rose in his eyes, only to fall abruptly away. 'Felicity and I moved too fast and it all fell apart. Damn it, you and I were pseudo-parents before we had a first date! This time there's a child involved, which makes it all the more reason *not* to rush things. I'm not going down that path again.'

'But I'm not Felicity.' She straightened her shoulders. 'Think of what we've shared in these past few weeks. You and I have been a more of a couple than you and Felicity ever were. It's been a real partnership.'

His cheeks hollowed. 'A partnership of necessity.'

His words burned like the burning cold of dry ice. She swallowed hard, trying to maintain her composure.

He tugged at his hair. 'Look, Tess, you're wonderful. You're an amazing doctor, you're beautiful, you've been the best surrogate mother Oscar could have, and this last week has been special, but we don't belong together.'

Curtis had told her the same thing. She'd been useful but now her time was up. Her throat clogged with words she could hardly get out, but she gave it one last attempt. 'I believe we do belong together.'

His expression filled with dismay mixed with sympathy. 'No. We don't. I belong working overseas and you belong in research. We have gifts that belong to the world, not just us. We can't be selfish.'

She took the full brunt of his words and knew she was down for the count. He'd summarily reduced the best moments of her life down to a measly *special* and she couldn't fight that. She couldn't make him love her and she wasn't going to plead, but she was dammed if she'd let him get off scot-free in regards to his nephew.

Holding herself together by a thread, she spoke from the heart. 'You've tied yourself up so tightly with this sense of duty it's strangling you. Yes, you have great skills and you have given a large chunk of your life to service. But in the process you lost your brother and you lost part of yourself.' She pushed on, ignoring the twitch in his jaw.

'Don't lose Oscar. He deserves more than duty. More than snatches of your time, more than just squeezing him in around dazzling saves and exciting surgery.'

His body went rigid and his words came out hard and cold. 'I have a plan that will work. I know what I'm doing.'

She pushed open the gate, the pain inside her building to the point of explosion, but she refused to cry in front him. 'No, Callum. I don't think you do.'

She turned away, her heart bleeding but knowing there was nothing else to be said.

Callum's small black case stood on the parquet entrance of his parents' Melbourne home. He travelled light because for the two-month rotation with Frontline he basically lived in scrubs, there being no real time off. He normally felt pumped and excited, knowing he was heading out to a Frontline mission, but this time everything was different. He still had the usual simmering of anticipation in his veins but he also had a lead weight sitting heavily in his gut. It had sat there for three days and he was ignoring it. He was committed to Frontline Aid and his work there was vital.

He rechecked his watch and sighed. He had six hours before he had to leave for Melbourne Airport.

Six hours and nothing to do. Oscar's care had successfully been transferred to his parents and Vanessa. James's estate was in the hands of the lawyers and Dr Turnington was making arrangements to buy the practice in Narranbool, finance pending. Everything had been wrapped up and he was leaving knowing there were no loose ends or unsolved problems.

Except Tess.

As much as he tried not to think about their conversation three days ago, he kept replaying it in his head. He hated it that she'd been hurt. Hell, he'd never meant to hurt her or to have her fall in love with him. He'd thought their holiday fling had been just that—a wonderful diversion before they resumed their lives and took up their plans.

Except, just like James, she'd changed the rules.

Since her proposal, he'd only seen her from a distance, delivering frozen breast milk to the east wing for Oscar. His mother had mentioned in passing that she was currently up at Narranbool, packing so she could move down and find a place to live in Melbourne.

But knowing she was in Narranbool and in the cottage they'd shared was doing his head in. His thoughts kept wandering to her, picturing her leaning against the solid redwood table, sipping her Earl Grey tea, conversing with the cat as she fed him, and cuddled up on the couch with her feet tucked under her, with Oscar in her arms.

But no matter how many images his brain kept flashing up, he knew down to his deepest point that he and Tess as a couple would not work. He knew that as intimately as night followed day. He'd been down that 'too-fast' relationship road before and one of them had to be the sensible one. One of them had to prevent a rancorous mess, and it had to be him.

And yet you've never been more content in your life than you have in the last few weeks.

He refused to listen to his wayward subconscious. He dealt in facts, not feelings. It was a hell of a lot safer.

'Mr Halroyd.' Vanessa, Oscar's nanny, came down the stairs carrying Oscar, her face creased with worry. 'I know that you're preparing to leave but with your parents not due back from Roseport for three hours, I need a bit of advice. Oscar's very unsettled and far more snuffly than yesterday, and he's just refused his bottle.'

Oscar had developed a cold and a cough the day Tess had left, and the last two nights Cal had spent more time walking the floor with an irritable and un-settled baby than asleep in bed. 'Do you want me to try? I managed to coax half a bottle into him at five a.m.'

'Yes, please.' She handed a quiet Oscar to Callum and followed them both into the library.

He cuddled the baby. 'Hey, buddy, feeling lousy? A cold can do that.'

Oscar cheeks were flushed and he gave a short cry against Cal's shoulder and then stopped.

Cradling Oscar, he sat in the reclining rocker and accepted the warmed expressed breast milk from Vanessa. He lifted the bottle to Oscar's lips and the baby accepted the teat, but a moment later he pulled away, whimpering, his breathing sounding raspy.

'That's what he was doing with me, poor little guy. It's like he's all blocked up and can't breathe and feed at the same time.' She stroked Oscar's head. 'I gave him some salt-water nasal drops to clear the congestion in his nose but although it helped yesterday, it hasn't today. I think his fontanelle is a bit sunken too, don't you?'

Cal put the bottle down on the table and laid his nephew on his lap, unwrapping the constricting bunny rug. Oscar's eyes, usually so alert and bright, stared dully and his nostrils flared as he took each breath.

A wave of anxiety thudded through Cal as he ripped open the snap buttons on Oscar's growsuit and pushed up his singlet. Oscar's tiny chest heaved with the effort of each breath and his respirations were shallow, rapid and increasingly noisy. Cal put his fingers on his chest, feeling the baby's tiny heart fluttering rapidly against the baby's chest. Oscar had deteriorated from a baby with the sniffles to being very ill in four short hours.

Fear unlike anything he'd ever known drilled through him. 'Get my medical bag.'

The edge in his voice sent Vanessa racing to the foyer.

Cal put his lips on Oscar's forehead, feeling the heat of a febrile baby, confirming how unwell he really was.

'Here.' Vanessa put the bag down next to him and opened it. 'What do you want?'

'My stethoscope and the ear thermometer. You take Oscar's temperature and I'll listen to his chest.'

A moment later his stethoscope was in his ears and he listened to Oscar's air entry between whimpering cries. With each breath he detected a wheeze as air tried to move past constricted airways. Every ounce of energy the baby had he was using it to breathe.

Oscar's limp and exhausted body terrified Cal and his automatic reaction was to turn to Tess, to see her serene smile and seek reassurance that he was panicking and Oscar wasn't really as sick as he thought he was.

But Tess wasn't there. He'd sent her away.

'Mr Halroyd?' Vanessa's scared voice broke into his thoughts.

'Call an ambulance, Vanessa. Now!'

Callum had been told to wait outside the paediatric ward and that the registrar would be out to speak to him soon. He'd told Vanessa to go and buy coffee, not because he wanted one but because he needed to be on his own.

Oscar, fight. He'd never felt so helpless as he had when he'd held his darling baby boy, knowing that every breath was an exhausting effort. He wanted to be in the ward, he wanted to see what was happening, but this time he was the relative, not the doctor.

Surely he gave people more information than he'd been given?

Until Narranbool, you used to avoid the relatives.

He shoved his hands deep into his pockets and paced up and down, stopping every now and then to peer through the door, but he couldn't see much. Just the backs of the staff and rows of cots.

He suddenly heard the unfamiliar thudding sound of running feet. He swung back to the door. Running in hospital was against all the rules unless…

The PA announced a code blue. *Cardiac arrest.*

His heart stalled as his chest muscles cramped. Ignoring all instructions, he pushed open the swing door of the ward and marched in.

A nurse immediately stepped forward, stopping him. 'Mr Halroyd, we need you to wait a bit longer.'

He drew himself up to his most imposing six feet two. 'I heard a code blue and—'

She put her hand on his arm and inclined her head toward a group of medical staff. 'It's not Oscar.' She bit her lip. 'It's a little six-month-old baby who was transferred down here. Poor little mite. He's been struggling with gastro and bronchiolitis but he has few reserves.'

Not Oscar. Relief collided with guilt for the other desperately ill baby.

'It's not fair, is it? Some kids have a much tougher start in life.' She gently pushed him back toward the door. 'I promise I will come and get you as soon as the doctors have finished examining Oscar.'

He wanted to pull rank, he wanted to stamp his foot, he wanted...

He wanted Oscar to be well and safe in his arms again.

The ripping sound of packing tape rolling off the dispenser and across the top of cardboard echoed around the cottage. Tess gripped the hand-held device and whipped it over box after box, sealing up the contents ready for the movers. She wished her heart could be sealed up as easily.

She'd rushed back to Narranbool the day after Callum had told her he didn't love her, telling Jennifer she needed to pack. It was the truth but, more accurately, she'd left then because she hadn't been able to bear to be in the same space as Callum and constantly reminded that he didn't love her.

So she'd turned off her phone and run away.

She tossed the red dispenser onto the couch and marched into the kitchen, plugging in the kettle. She'd thought coming back to Narranbool for a couple of days might help. How wrong could a woman be? Every corner of the house held a memory of laughter, of companionship, of intellectual conversation mixed with equal parts of silliness, and all of it taunted her, reminding her of everything that she'd lost.

A loud bang on the door roused her and she padded over in her bare feet. Opening the door, she faced a burly mover. 'Oh, hello, I wasn't expecting you until this afternoon.'

'It's 12.05, love, that's afternoon in my book.' He shook his head. 'If you'd checked your messages you would have known the time got moved.' He walked into the lounge room. 'Still, looks like you're ready for me.'

Feeling behind in the information stakes, Tess covered. 'Yes, that's them all ready. I'll leave you to it.' She returned to the kitchen and found her tote bag where she'd dropped it on a chair soon after arriving two nights ago. Doubting she'd missed anything really important, but chastened by the mover, she located her phone at the bottom of the bag and switched it on.

She watched the bars load up as the phone connected to the network and then it beeped once. Then it beeped a second time and a third, until it was just one long, continuous electronic noise.

Ten messages from Callum.

Ten messages she didn't want to open. She glanced at the clock. He'd be getting ready to leave for the airport, to leave the country. To leave her.

He's already left you.

Although she longed to hear his voice again, she had no intention of hearing a 'Goodbye and all the best with the rest of your life' message. She placed the phone on the table and poured her tea.

As she sipped the hot brew, her eyes strayed to the phone. Ten messages. That was a lot of messages. No one sent ten 'Goodbye and all the best with the rest of your life' messages.

She put down her mug and slowly picked up the phone, steeling herself to activate the voicemail.

Callum's controlled voice sounded down the line, becoming increasingly frayed with each message, until his frantic voice shredded her heart into a million pieces.

CHAPTER TWELVE

'CALLUM.'

On hearing his mother's voice, he turned away from the cot where his beloved nephew battled to breathe. Oxygen poured into a Perspex box, which was placed over Oscar's head, helping to raise the oxygen saturation of his blood.

Jennifer crossed the special-care nursery and walked toward him, her face pale. She only used his full name when he was in trouble or she was upset. 'We left Roseport the moment we got your frantic message.'

'Mum.' His anxiety for Oscar compounded his concern for his mother's health and he immediately put his arms around her, wanting reassurance. Shock trailed through him at his need to touch someone. James had been the hugger in the family, not him.

You hugged Tess more in three weeks than you've hugged anyone in your life.

But Tess was in Narranbool, a thousand kilometres away. He desperately wanted her here at the hospital for Oscar.

You want her too. You need her.

But her phone was switched off and all he'd been able to do had been to leave messages. Ten messages.

His mother's anxious eyes sought Oscar. 'He's so tiny against all that equipment. How is he?'

Cal ran his hand through his hair, thinking about the last three hours. 'He's doing much better with the oxygen and the IV fluids to rehydrate him. The staff are very confident that in twenty-four hours he'll probably be back to feeding himself and the drip will come out.' He looked beyond his mother. 'Where's Dad?'

'He's collecting— He's on his way.' She glanced at him. 'Tell me what exactly is wrong with Oscar.'

'He's got something called bronchiolitis. The virus that caused his cold has made all his airways narrow and he's having trouble breathing.'

'A slight cold can do that?' Jennifer's expression held disbelief.

'It can when you're only a few weeks old or if you're malnourished, like—'

She threw him an accusatory glance. 'Perhaps insisting that Tess wean him was not a good idea.'

He snapped. 'Oscar's not malnourished! He's been getting expressed breast milk. I was talking about the baby who had to be transferred to ICU.' Guilt clawed at him again from two fronts but a need to defend his behaviour reared its head. 'Tess never signed on to be a full-time mother to Oscar. All I did was relieve her of her obligation so she could get on with her life.'

His mother's blue eyes sparked. 'I think if you're honest with yourself, Callum, you'll find you did what *you* thought was best so you could get on with yours.'

Her words scorched him. 'I did what was best for

everyone.' But his words sounded hollow. Oscar was battling to breathe, his mother was obviously furious with him and Tess was hours away, avoiding him until he left town. For the first time in his life all his carefully controlled plans were unravelling like wool pulled from a knitting needle.

'What time do you leave for the airport?'

Her words stunned him. He couldn't believe his mother thought he would leave on his scheduled flight. 'Do you honestly think I would leave today with Oscar so sick?'

'We know your job is important to you, which is why you have set everything up so you can come and go.' She crossed her arms. 'Oscar could get sick at any time in the two-month period that you will be away, just like he could be sick during the two-month period you will be home. Children don't work around schedules, Callum.' She sat down facing Oscar, turning her back to him.

Stunned at his mother's response, he turned at the squeak of the ward door opening. His father, looking unfamiliar in a hospital gown, ushered in another gown-clad visitor.

Tess.

His heart soared. *Thank you, Dad*. His father must have organised for Tess to be flown down from Narranbool. Everything would be all right now that Tess was there.

In three long strides he was by her side, wrapping his arms around her, inhaling the sweet scent of coconut, the tangy scent of citrus and absorbing her wondrous heat. Holding her rammed home how much he'd missed her and peace settled around his heart. This felt so…right, holding the woman he loved.

Loved.

He waited for the panic to come, for all the familiar and well-worn excuses to pile up, but nothing happened. Tess was nothing like Felicity and lack of time had nothing to do with love.

It was that simple—he loved Tess.

Burying his face in her silky hair, he pulled her close and whispered, 'We need you, Tess.'

She stiffened in his arms and immediately stepped back, breaking all contact and keeping her gaze fixed over his shoulder. 'I came for Oscar and your parents.' She walked around him, straight over to Jennifer.

The quietly spoken words carried the punch of an electric shock. He turned around slowly and then stood stock-still, watching as his parents embraced Tess. Watching them gather around Oscar's cot, a unified team. A family.

A family he felt completely shut out of.

A family he had for so long turned his back on because he'd believed others needed him more. Now they'd turned their back on him.

You lost your brother and you lost part of yourself. Tess's insightful words echoed in his head with frightening accuracy. He'd pushed James away and now he was gone. He'd rationalised that he could be a half-time father to Oscar and that would be OK. Now, on top of everything else, unless he acted quickly he'd lose the woman he loved.

The thought of that sucked all the air from his lungs.

The preset reminder on his watch that he'd set early

this morning bleeped, telling him it was time to leave for the airport. He pressed the 'off' button with a hard jerk, silencing it. Suddenly everything that he'd valued, everything that had been so very important six hours ago, crumbled to a smoking pile of ashes.

He'd been an utter fool. A blind and conceited fool. He'd convinced himself he was saving the world but in reality he'd been hiding. James had been so far ahead of him in knowing what was important in life. James had been connected to people and places in a way he'd never known. *Except for the last few weeks.*

But how could he fix this? How could he convince Tess he loved her and they belonged together? His mind spun as the flash of images from his time in Narranbool mixed in with verbal sound bites. Slowly from the ashes of his former life rose a new phoenix and his path was crystal clear.

The lights in the paediatric ward were turned down low, a concession to the fact it was dark outside although the hospital staff worked on irrespective of day and time. Tess cuddled Oscar for a few minutes, loving the feel of him in her arms. She hated the tape on his tiny cheek that held the nasal oxygen prongs in place but she gave thanks that it meant he was well enough now to be out of the head box and she could hold him.

Oscar's hand gripped her forefinger, a great sign he was improving. She was there for Oscar and she kept telling herself that to keep her thoughts from wandering to Callum. The feel of his arms around her when she'd arrived had almost undone her resolve to hold herself together and hold herself apart from him. The desire to fling her arms around his neck and snuggle in against his chest had almost swamped her.

We need you, Tess.

Four short words had punctured her heart and steeled her resolve. He only needed her because Oscar was sick. She was the woman needed for the breast milk she could provide. Needed but not loved. Able to be discarded when she was no longer required.

Well, she would always be there for Oscar and somehow she'd learn to deal with her feelings for Callum. Thankfully with him overseas for half of the year she wouldn't have to see much of him. Just like she hadn't seen much of him in the ten hours since she'd arrived.

Once Oscar had stabilised, Callum had been in and out of the paediatric ward, taking phone calls, and she'd heard his phone beeping almost continuously with the sound of incoming messages. She supposed he was re-organising his departure.

The nurse walked over. 'It's amazing how fast they improve. Would you like to try and breastfeed him?'

'Yes, please.' The older Halroyds and Vanessa had gone home to catch some sleep but Tess wasn't leaving. Three days without Oscar had been three days too long.

She unlatched her bra, her breasts heavy and aching with milk, and gently expressed a few drops of milk onto the tip of her nipple. Positioning Oscar, she held her breath, wondering if he would be able to suck and breathe at the same time.

He quickly attached, sucking well for a few moments before pulling off. 'Well done, little man. Do you want to try again?'

She tickled her nipple against his lips and slowly but surely, with little breaks, Oscar managed to empty her breast. She wanted to high five someone in delight.

'That's a sight for sore eyes.'

She stilled at Cal's voice. Once she would have gloried in hearing its rich, melodic tones. Now the sound just reminded her that she was useful but not loved.

She didn't look up. 'He's being weaned off oxygen and if he keeps up with the feeding the drip will be out by morning.'

'He went down so fast and gave me one hell of a scare.' Callum squatted down next to the chair, his hand stroking Oscar's head. 'Thanks for coming. Thanks for giving him what he needs so much.'

She didn't want to do this. She didn't want to chat and pretend that there wasn't this huge thing between them. An unbridgeable gulf of different wants and needs. 'I'll always be here for Oscar.'

'I know.'

His heartfelt words tore at the flimsy scab that had barely formed over her heart.

The nurse returned and lifted the sleeping Oscar from Tess's arms. 'He needs to rest and you two need to take a break as well.' Her face took on a stern and uncompromising expression. 'We don't want to see you back here in under an hour.'

Callum stood up. 'Come on, you need cake and coffee, and I know a place in Lygon Street that will be serving even though it's two a.m.' He extended his hand to help her up from the recliner.

She stared at his broad hand, at his long, strong,

talented fingers—fingers that performed amazing surgery and had elicited the most wondrous sensations in her body, sensations that had taken her places she'd never known existed.

Don't hold his hand. Don't make it harder on yourself.

'Tess, it's just coffee. Please.'

He'd read her mind. She glanced up into grey eyes, expecting to see the usual combination of controlled emotions, but instead she met a swirling melee of them.

Her heart lurched. She could refuse the controlled man and controlling doctor. But she couldn't refuse the hurting man.

Red lamps glowed, imbuing a warmth and welcome in the long, narrow café as the bar staff upended tables and chairs and wiped down the long, wooden bar, preparing to close up after a long day. Tess thought they would have refused to serve them but one smile from Callum and the young waitress had eagerly delivered his coffee and her hot chocolate, along with a huge slab of lemon tart. They sat at the back, facing each other—Callum in a chair and she on a couch, with a small table between them.

Tess stirred in two white marshmallows, watching them slowly decrease in size as the sugary confection melted into the creamy chocolate. The short trip by car to the café had been silent. What was left to say to a man who had told her theirs was only a partnership of necessity?

Nothing at all. She lifted the heavy white mug to her lips and sipped.

'It's good, isn't it?'

So this was what it had come to—talking about food. 'It is.' She continued drinking.

The silence hung between them while they both drank.

Callum finally broke it. 'Mavis Cooper sends her love to you and Oscar.'

The unexpected words startled her. 'Mavis? How do you know that?'

He shrugged. 'She texted me.'

Tess blinked with surprise. 'Mavis has a mobile?'

He gave a wry smile. 'I think she used Betty's. Gerry Gibson also contacted me and passed on his and Ruth's best wishes for a speedy recovery. Seems Oscar's won a few hearts in Narranbool, as have you.'

Her mind grappled with the fact that the people she'd said goodbye to only the previous morning had contacted Callum and not her. 'I'm surprised that they—' She bit off the rest of the sentence. Being rude to Callum wasn't going to gain her anything.

'Surprised they contacted me?' He nodded, his expression serious. 'Fair point. I've not exactly been fair to Narranbool, but I was their doctor for a couple of weeks.' He gave her an accusatory look. 'They probably would have contacted you but you seem to have taken to turning off your phone.'

'Touché.' She leaned back on the couch and picked up a magazine that had been left there. 'Callum, I don't want to sit here and make polite conversation with you. You made your stance perfectly clear at Westwinds and there's nothing left for us to say to each other.'

'That's where you're wrong.'

Her hand stalled on the magazine page and in the half-light of the café she caught an unfamiliar earnest expression cross his face. *Don't fall for it. He'll only ask you for something.*

But the tenseness in his expression called to her. Trying to still her hammering heart, she slowly laid the magazine back on the couch cushion and breathed in deeply so that her voice wouldn't waver. 'Do you have something you want to say to me?'

'I do.'

She steeled herself for more pain.

He moved to the couch, sitting down next to her. 'Tess, I've been a conceited fool.'

His musky scent enveloped her, dragging at her resistance. 'If it's absolution you're after before you leave for Frontline, I can't give it to you.'

He took her verbal hit with barely a flinch. 'That's not what I want. I want you.'

I want you. The unexpected words bounced around her brain, unable to be absorbed. *A partnership of necessity.* She swallowed hard, gearing up for the request she'd known would come. 'I can't be your handy girl, Callum. I can't be the person you call on when you need something. I can't do that and it's not fair of you to ask.'

He reached out his hand and brushed her hair from her eyes. 'I want you, Tess, because I love you.'

His wondrous touch combined with his words, and her mind blanked. Reaching for his hand, she closed her fingers around his and pulled his hand away so she could try and think. Try and understand. 'You love me?' Disbelief pounded her. 'Don't confuse need with love. How…how can you love me when three days ago you didn't?'

'I loved you then, I just didn't know it.' His free hand covered hers as remorse streaked across his face. 'I'm so sorry that I've hurt you. If I could turn back time, I would do things so very differently.'

He loves me. Her breath came in short, sharp gasps as she tried to make sense of this. 'What…? How would you do things differently?'

'For a start I would have listened to James. He knew far more than I did. He knew that the love of a good woman and the love of family is what makes everything worthwhile. He knew he could have all of that and still be working for the greater good.'

He tilted her chin with a feather-light touch, forcing her to look at him. 'You make my life worthwhile, Tess. You and Oscar.'

Joy cascaded through her but the niggling voice inside her head wasn't quite ready to be silenced. 'For years you've lived for work, for the high-octane excitement of surgery in war-torn nations, doing what you so passionately believe in.' She took in a long breath, knowing this to be a crunch moment. 'Oscar and I want you to be happy but we don't want to play second fiddle to Frontline.'

He nodded, understanding clear in his eyes. 'And you won't. I've resigned.'

She started to shake with shock. 'Resigned? But your job is so much a part of who you are.'

'And it still will be.' He tilted his head, his gaze questioning. 'I thought you'd be happy that I resigned.'

Thoughts jumbled in her head, falling over each

other before they could be fully processed. Callum Halroyd loved her. He'd quit his job for her. He wanted to be a family with her and Oscar and she should be over the moon.

But she needed something more and she gripped both his hands. 'This is only going to work if we are a true partnership. That means we support each other, which is very different from doing what we think the other person wants.'

'Tess, I want you—that's a given.' He smiled at her, a knowing smile. 'I've learned more about myself in a short time with you than I have in my whole life. James tried to show me what was important but I was blind to the message. You managed to take the blinkers away and open my eyes. You showed me my twin brother hadn't settled—hell, he'd been trail blazing. And I want to continue his work.'

'In Narranbool?' She could hardly believe what he was saying. 'Cal, as much as I want to live in Narranbool, I just don't see it working for you.'

He grinned. 'You know me so well. I don't want to be the Narranbool GP. I'll leave that to you and Leo Turnington that is, if you still want to be Narranbool's GP? If you want to do research, well, we'll work around it.'

Her heart sang. 'I would love to be a part-time GP in Narranbool. But what are you planning on doing?'

'Frontline stuff a lot closer to home. I want to get involved in indigenous health and extend what you and James have started. So many of those kids I saw that day at the settlement needed ENT surgery. That little baby today rammed it all home. Our little Oscar is sick but he's so much healthier than them and he'll fight the bronchiolitis. Those kids need the same access to clean water and health as we have.'

Excitement peppered his face. 'I've got the surgical contacts for creating flying squads to remote areas and Dad has the ear of some pretty high-up government officials. I'm applying for surgical privileges at Mildura Base and I'm hoping with government funding to ramp up Narranbool Hospital so a lot of the simple stuff can be done there. Mildura is too far away for families to have to travel.'

Her action man had been in big-time planning mode. He was still saving the world but a bit closer to home. 'It all sounds wonderful, but how are you going to manage spreading yourself out over a huge geographical area?'

His voice deepened with emotion. 'I'm *not* missing out on Oscar growing up, Tess. I want to be there when he says his first word and I want to see him walk and I want to stand out on the Narranbool oval and teach him how to kick a footy.'

He put his arm around her waist. 'I'll still be operating, but not as much. A lot of my work will be organising and lobbying, and I can do that from Narranbool. I've spoken to Dad and we're taking advantage of the Halroyd wealth. Instead of a car, I'm getting a plane so I can be home every night.'

She gazed up at him, thrilled that he'd covered all the important points. 'You've thought it all through.'

'I have.' His eyes zeroed in on her. 'Do you think I've missed something?'

She asked the final nagging question. 'Action man,

are you sure you don't want to do one rotation a year with Frontline?'

Appreciation filled his face. 'Thank you, but sometimes it's time to move on, and this is one of those times.' He pulled her close, his grey eyes mostly lit with anticipation but tinged with a hint of uncertainty. 'So, how does that all sound, Tess? Does it sound like the sort of partnership you want to be in?'

She thought her heart would explode with happiness. 'Yes, that is exactly the sort of partnership I want to be in. A partnership with you. You, Oscar and—'

'A tribe of Halroyds?' Hope lined his face.

She laughed. 'I don't know if I have any twins on my side of the family but it will be fun finding out.'

He grinned. 'I can't wait.' His expression slowly became reflective. 'You know, when James and I were little, whenever we had an argument over a toy we used to consult our imaginary friend, Oscar. He'd decide the verdict and over time he solved a lot of disputes.' Cal wound his finger around her hair, his voice suddenly thick. 'I can't help but think James wanted to call his son Oscar because he believed his arrival in the world could bring us back together.'

She stroked his face. 'And it has. I'm sure he knows.'

He nodded and suddenly stood up, pulling her to her feet. 'Will you marry me, Tess?'

She leaned forward wrapping her arms around his neck and gazed up into his loving face. 'Yes, please.'

His wide grin of pleasure hovered on his face and then he kissed her. A long, hard, bone-melting kiss that promised love, commitment, compromise and laughter.

EPILOGUE

THE first pink rays of the sun rose over Westwinds, the dawn bringing a new day and new hope. Tess faced the sky, snuggled into her husband's chest. His loving arms circled her, warding off the chill of an autumn morning that nipped at any bare skin.

'Mummy, Daddy, do you think he's come?' An excited Oscar tugged on their arms.

Patrick stepped forward and swung his four-year-old grandson up into his arms. 'It won't be long now but you must wait until the sun is completely up, mate, or you'll miss the eggs the Easter Bunny's left in the garden.'

'Eggs!' Two-year-old Bridget squealed, and started to run around in a circle on the spongy buffalo-grass lawn.

Her more sedate twin sister, Lily, stayed cuddled up to her grandmother, a hopeful expression on her face. 'See Bunny?'

Jennifer set her down and caught hold of Bridget's hand. 'Let's go and look, shall we?' She led the twins down one of the 'magic' paths in her garden that the children believed was full of fairies and kindly goblins.

'Come on, Granddad,' Oscar implored. 'Put me down. We can't let the girls get them all.'

Patrick roared with laughter and obliged, before jogging after Oscar and quickly disappearing from view.

'That just leaves you and me.' Cal's arms tightened around Tess. 'Happy?'

Every year for four years the Halroyds had gathered at Westwinds for Easter, one of the many family traditions that Tess cherished. Her foster-family had even made it down one year to share the celebration they'd introduced to her so many years ago.

She turned in Cal's arms to face him. 'I never believed I could be this happy. I have the family I always dreamed of.'

'You dreamed of Bridget discovering how to use a red felt pen?'

'Not exactly, no. It's true, I would have preferred her artistic skills to be on paper rather than the kitchen wall. That child of yours has the Halroyd determination.'

Cal laughed. 'Why is it that they're my children when they do something naughty but you take all the credit when they do something brilliant?'

'A mother's prerogative.'

He raised a dark brow. 'Is that so? Well, it's a father's prerogative to go sailing and leave the mother alone to deal with children hyped on Easter chocolate.'

She grinned, knowing he was teasing her. She and Callum were a team, whether at work or at home. A true partnership. 'Actually, I thought we might both go sailing and leave Vanessa and your parents to deal with over-excited children.'

'Excellent plan but, sadly, not remotely possible. We are responsible parents after all.' His grey eyes suddenly darkened with desire and he tucked some stray hair behind her ear. 'Still, the garden is pretty big and they're going to be tied up on this hunt for quite some time.'

After four years it still only took one look from Cal and need thrummed through her. 'Perhaps we should go down to the boat shed and just check everything's in shipshape order. You know, make sure the roof hasn't sprung a leak, check that the engine on the powerboat will start.' She shot him her best sultry look. 'And test the springs on the old couch.'

'Did I tell you that I love you, Tess Halroyd?'

'Every single day.' She wrapped her arms around his neck and pulled his lips down to hers, pledging her love and giving thanks for his.

THREE POWERFUL SEXY MEN WHO CAN'T BE TAMED…

THE HIGH-SOCIETY WIFE
by Helen Bianchin

THE BILLIONAIRE BOSS'S FORBIDDEN MISTRESS
by Miranda Lee

THE SECRET BABY REVENGE
by Emma Darcy

Available 15th May 2009

www.millsandboon.co.uk

M&B

FREE

2 BOOKS AND A SURPRISE GIFT!

We would like to take this opportunity to thank you for reading this Mills & Boon® book by offering you the chance to take TWO more specially selected titles from the Medical™ series absolutely FREE! We're also making this offer to introduce you to the benefits of the Mills & Boon® Book Club™—

- ★ **FREE home delivery**
- ★ **FREE gifts and competitions**
- ★ **FREE monthly Newsletter**
- ★ **Books available before they're in the shops**
- ★ **Exclusive Mills & Boon Book Club offers**

Accepting these FREE books and gift places you under no obligation to buy; you may cancel at any time, even after receiving your free shipment. Simply complete your details below and return the entire page to the address below. You don't even need a stamp!

YES! Please send me 2 free Medical books and a surprise gift. I understand that unless you hear from me, I will receive 4 superb new titles every month for just £2.99 each, postage and packing free. I am under no obligation to purchase any books and may cancel my subscription at any time. The free books and gift will be mine to keep in any case.

M9ZEE

Ms/Mrs/Miss/Mr...Initials ....
BLOCK CAPITALS PLEASE

Surname ....

Address ....

....

....Postcode ....

Send this whole page to:
The Mills & Boon Book Club, FREEPOST CN81, Croydon, CR9 3WZ